About the Author

Cyle Tramel is a seasoned traveler with a passion for cultural exploration and storytelling. He believes that everyone has a story to tell and that every story, no matter how unbelievable, deserves to be told. This is his first book.

Cyle Tramel

DETECTIVE RAY SHIELDS AND THE MOUNTAIN OF TRIAL

AUSTIN MACAULEY PUBLISHERS™

LONDON · CAMBRIDGE · NEW YORK · SHARJAH

Copyright © Cyle Tramel 2024

All rights reserved. No part of this publication may be reproduced, distributed, or transmitted in any form or by any means, including photocopying, recording, or other electronic or mechanical methods, without the prior written permission of the publisher, except in the case of brief quotations embodied in critical reviews and certain other non-commercial uses permitted by copyright law. For permission requests, write to the publisher.

Any person who commits any unauthorized act in relation to this publication may be liable to criminal prosecution and civil claims for damages.

This is a work of fiction. Names, characters, businesses, places, events, locales, and incidents are either the products of the author's imagination or used in a fictitious manner. Any resemblance to actual persons, living or dead, or actual events is purely coincidental.

Ordering Information
Quantity sales: Special discounts are available on quantity purchases by corporations, associations, and others. For details, contact the publisher at the address below.

Publisher's Cataloging-in-Publication data
Tramel, Cyle
Detective Ray Shields and the Mountain of Trial

ISBN 9798889103943 (Paperback)
ISBN 9798889103950 (Hardback)
ISBN 9798889103974 (ePub e-book)
ISBN 9798889103967 (Audiobook)

Library of Congress Control Number: 2023917459

www.austinmacauley.com/us

First Published 2024
Austin Macauley Publishers LLC
40 Wall Street, 33rd Floor, Suite 3302
New York, NY 10005
USA

mail-usa@austinmacauley.com
+1 (646) 5125767

Acknowledgement

I must start by thanking my former student, Raj, for providing the initial inspiration that would lead to the writing of this book. Look what you made me do, my friend.

Heather and Trish, thank you so very much for your investment in my confidence. You never once let me falter and for that, I thank you.

Most importantly, I owe a great deal of thanks to the woman who has had to tolerate every 'what do you think about this word?' and 'do you think this sounds good?' that I dished out. And let us not forget, 'Will you please read this and tell me what you think?' My dear, your patience knows no end. Thank you.

Prologue

The tiny bell that hung above the front door to the diner rang softly as its only other inhabitants made their way out. For some reason, the rhythmic jingle of the bell came as a distraction to me following the door's closure, and it was a welcomed disruption to my current thoughts. "They should be here soon," I said to myself, sighing as I looked up at an empty table.

Outside, a few stray dogs nosed through the garbage across the empty street. They didn't seem to mind the rain all that much, and come to think of it, neither did I. In fact, the day Laura and I first encountered each other, I had just stepped through the door of my office, the sky pouring down across the city much like it was today.

"I need your help, detective," she had said to me, the smoke from the cigarette she held only just beginning to dissipate. "My name is Laura DuPont, and I think someone has been watching me."

I recalled that all the features of her face were in perfect harmony with each other that night, all except for her eyes. They were a very unfamiliar shade of blue. She appeared to be well-composed and carried herself with an elegant posture, and yet, I could still see the exhaustion. The gentleness that had captivated my attention seemed limited, and in her eyes, I could see there was genuine suffering.

"Please, why don't you have a seat?" I gestured for her to take a seat on the sofa that doubled both as office furniture and as a place to lay my head during some of the more consuming cases that I handled. Instead, she chose to sit on a curved chair near the window, her face illuminated by what little light made its way through the shutters. The room had grown silent while she situated herself, and when she realized the mistake that she had made in her choice of furniture, she straightened in an attempt to get comfortable. The chair had been a gift from a somewhat eccentric client of mine and really served no purpose other than raising the status of my office decorum.

Having faced that same struggle many times over, I smirked at the unfolding scenario of discomfort in front of me, before taking a seat across from her. "Ms. DuPont, why don't you go ahead and tell me a little about this stalker of yours. Is it someone you work with, perhaps someone from a place you frequently visit?"

"No, no, it's nothing like that at all Mr. Shields."

"It's Ray. Please call me Ray." She nodded in agreement with the suggestion and let herself relax enough to smile before continuing. "Well, the thing is I've never actually seen anyone, but I know that I'm being watched. Worst of all is that it never ends… I mean… it's day and night, and I just don't even know if…" She stopped short of finishing her sentence and nervously looked around the room. "I'm not even sure…" her voice tapered off, and it became clear that she didn't want to continue.

I resolved to relax my tone just a little before speaking again. "Laura, do you mind if I call you Laura?" I asked her. "Certainly," she responded.

"You're not sure about what exactly?" It had taken her another two drags of her cigarette to muster up the courage to speak. "I'm not sure they are even human."

Recalling this part of the conversation still creeped me out despite it having been years since she explained it to me.

"I know it sounds crazy, but I get these feelings sometimes, feelings that aren't normal. They can't be, and I don't want them. Something is making me have them, watching to see how they affect me, taking pleasure when they best me; it's like one's continuous presence." Her plea had been shaky and desperate, but more importantly, it was honest. So, I had decided to help her. I was about to inform her of my rates when she promptly spoke up, declaring that she had no money and instead expressed her desire to work for me as a form of payment.

The memory of that moment briefly amused me, and I cracked a smile before my attention was brought back to the front of the diner as the bell rang for a second time. I didn't have to look at the door to know who it was; I could practically smell the bar walk in from the rain with him. Eddie had arrived.

Being a self-made man, Eddie didn't take kindly to orders. More importantly, the man didn't like being told that he couldn't carry a gun. So, his reaction was less than desirable when I asked him to meet me at the quaint diner unarmed and sober. I could see that he was still pouting as he ignored my gesture of greetings and sat down with a rather loud thud. "How you doing, Eddie?" I asked, offering him a menu. "What's so damn important that it couldn't wait until tomorrow?" Even though he smelled awful and could undoubtedly be found with a tin of jack tucked away in his jacket, he was most definitely not drunk. "Eddie," I said, "this morning, someone tried to have me killed."

"Killed? Are you kidding me, boss? Someone comes gunning for you, and the first thing you do is call me and ask me to meet you unarmed. What's gotten into you?" Eddie's words came to a halt, and at the realization that I had asked him to come unarmed as a precaution against the possibility that he was responsible for the attack, he adjusted his posture and spoke defensively.

"Now wait just a minute there, you don't think I went and set you up? Do you?"

The sound of screeching tires intruded in our conversation, and we both shifted our attention out the window. Outside, a dark brown Lincoln continental pulled up. The headlights dimmed as the vehicle turned off and then extinguished roughly at the same time that the door was flung open. Even here, in the late hours of the evening, she knew how to make an entrance. Laura hid under a fistful of newspaper as she made her way from the car to the front door. "The thought had crossed my mind," I said finally, before glancing up to see Laura walk in and toss the newspaper in the bin by the door.

Her hips swayed in their usual way as she walked through the empty diner towards us. Her gaze met mine, and for a moment, I thought I caught a glimpse of that same look of worry that she wore that distant rainy day. I suppose it would help to mention that I never discovered the source of Laura's fear. The presence that she spoke of stopped harassing her shortly after she came under my employment. So, we decided together that it must have been your average secret admirer who decided to skip town after discovering that she was now working for a private detective.

As she took her seat across from me, I could see her nose twitch involuntarily at the smell of alcohol that stained Eddie's Jacket. "You should at least consider dry cleaning Eddie." Her comment, justified as it was, didn't appear to appeal to him. "Now, why have you dragged me out here at such a distasteful hour?" she asked, shifting her attention from Eddie over to me.

Deciding not to delay the inevitable, I spoke bluntly. "Honestly, Laura, I…" I paused briefly, considering what I was about to ask her. Laura and Eddie were the closest thing to family that I had, and here I was seriously considering the idea that one of them could be behind my near death experience this morning. What was I thinking?

After a moment of staring down at the empty plate on the table that I had used to cover the coffee stains of the booth's previous occupants, I decided to withdraw my previous assumptions and instead settled on simply telling her what happened.

"Sorry," I said resentfully. "Look, this morning, I was following a lead at John Adams park when a man stepped out of the shadows, put a gun to my belly, and told me I shouldn't have checked the mail this morning."

Chapter 1

Waking like I did most mornings, legs propped up on the leather couch in my office, a file or two of current cases sprawled across the coffee table in front of me, and an empty mug still half in hand, I noted a lack of something that usually accompanied my morning routine. There was no coffee.

"Laura," I said, raising my head, expecting to see the silhouette of her neatly done updo through the milky glass window that separated my private office from the rest of the Ray Shields Detective Agency. There was no response. "That's unusual," I said, muttering as I got up from my place on the couch. No coffee and no response could only mean one thing, no Laura… and Laura was never late. With the exception of my birthday last year, she either beat me to the office, or she was here when I woke up.

Opening the door, I glanced around the larger room. Her desk was in impeccable dress save for her chair, which was pushed back and turned in its usual fashion, facing left. Laura liked it that way.

I had once asked her why she kept her desk so neat but never bothered to push her chair in, and she replied by telling me that her desk is tidy because everything has its place, and as for her chair, there was no sense in giving herself extra work.

I suppose she meant that if she sat in the chair, turned, and slid forward, it was all part of sitting down at one's desk, and if she pushed out and just left it that way, that her chair would be ready for her when she returned. Whatever the case, her way was her way, and it didn't interfere with her work.

Making my way to the front door, I could see that the mail was still in its place on the floor, and the door, while in desperate need of a new coat of paint, was still bolted shut. "Great, another one," I said, bending down to pick up the mail. The stack contained a few thank-you letters, the electric bill, and amidst the junk mail that the mailman never failed to deliver, there was an unmarked envelope.

Unfortunately, in my line of work, this was a common occurrence, and the contents could vary to being anything from an anonymous tip to the occasional threat of bodily harm or worse, death. Both of which could be attributed to what Eddie liked to believe as being a rather genius way of gathering information, boasting around bars local to the area where we were hired to do a job.

I received this kind of mail so frequently in fact, that I had gotten used to discerning between the two types of correspondence, and this envelope, while blank, carried with it the scent of a woman. Whoever made its delivery wore an expensive perfume and possibly too much of it.

"Well, no harm here," I said, and I began opening the envelope as I made my way back to my desk.

Once opened, two pictures crossed my eyes, one of a woman whose face was familiar to me and yet her identity currently unplaced, and the other of a relic of sorts in the shape of an M with a few extra extremities. I placed the two photographs to the side so that I could read the folded paper that had undoubtedly been placed last for effect.

"Keeping with little harm,
Your actions will determine
My own.
Open to a fair trade.
Now it's all on you."
11:15 John Adams Park—Alone

"What the hell is that supposed to mean?"

What the author of this note wanted was a complete mystery, but the message was clear. I was to meet at J.A. Park at 11:15, and if I failed to do so, this woman would likely suffer more than the trauma of being held captive.

Picking up one of the photographs, I began to look it over. The attire of the woman was suited for a lovely evening out. Her dress, while a pretty shade of white and pink, was covered in dirt, and her face, equally as filthy, showed a great deal of fear. The note may have indicated keeping with little harm, but the look on her face clearly told me that whoever it was that was holding her hostage meant what they said about my actions determining what would happen to her.

The setting itself was dark, and very little could be seen of the background.

"Damn," I muttered. I was hoping that there might have been a clue as to where she was being held, or at the very least, where the picture was taken, but there was nothing.

The lighting, however, did tell me that the photograph was taken at night, and considering how she was dressed it was easy to conclude that it was taken on the evening of her abduction.

The second picture was even less helpful. It was a black-and-white picture of a hand holding some sort of medallion, with the letter M imprinted on it. A line ran from the center of the M down about halfway and up again to the top edge of the medallion, and a single line extended from one side to the other directly through the medallion's center.

The medallion itself might have been gold or brass judging from the tone it took in this picture, and it seemed to be well-handled and was worn down quite a bit. The hand was light even in the darkness of the photograph, so the assailant most likely was very fair in complexion.

I noted that the angle the photograph was taken from would have been extremely difficult to accomplish one-handed, so it's possible the abductor wasn't the individual holding the medallion. This could only mean that whoever I was supposed to meet at the park was likely not alone.

Reaching into my desk drawer, I pulled out my spyglass. An ancient thing with a large brass ring encasing a convex lens and a mahogany wood handle complete with the initials R.S. It was a gift from my brother after solving my first case. Laura was constantly hounding me for not using the office computer, but I guess I found solace in doing it the old-fashioned way.

In today's day and age, it only takes a moment to scan a picture, and suddenly you have all the zoom you want at the scroll of a mouse wheel. Of course, that was an extra step in my eyes, so I guess you could say I was either too lazy or too stubborn to do it.

I began by concentrating my focus on the edges of one of the photographs, looking for even the slightest clue as to where these might have been taken. I swept the glass from left to right, perusing each of the pictures with great care, and after about twenty minutes, I sat the glass down and stood up, sighing at my failed attempt to gain any ground.

Looking at the clock, I noted the time. It was eight-thirty in the morning, and the park was nearly a forty-five-minute walk from here. If I leave now, I guess I'll have some time to case the park first.

"Another sound idea by the great detective Ray Shields," I said to myself while gathering my hat and old gabardine, Burberry trench coat from the coat rack before heading out the door.

Chapter 2

Laura awoke under the withering canopy of three rather large trees. Her vision was a bit fuzzy, and she wasn't altogether sure where she was. She sat in a state of confusion for a few minutes and looked around, trying to make sense of how she got here.

Last night was a blur. The last thing she could remember was sitting in her quaint two-bedroom brownstone, reading one of her father's copies of Essais de Montaigne. Her French was rusty since she didn't often have a chance to use it, and though she found the readings to be a bit archaic at times, Montaigne was quite brilliant, and at least this way, she kept her French up.

As she took to her feet and began to walk about under the shade provided by the canopy, she noticed something etched into the tree that she had been leaning against when she awoke.

Les simples & les ignorans, s'eslevent & se saisissent du ciel. "The simple ones—" she said, translating almost automatically into English. A habit she'd formed while trying to educate Ray in her language. Looking to her right, she realized the other tree had something etched into it as well. Stepping back, she read and translated again from the tree in front of her and then the next.

The simple ones, and the ignorant, rise and seize themselves from heaven, and we, with all our knowledge, plunge into a hellish abyss.

The words stood out to her. These were almost direct quotes from Montaigne, but given no context past these lines, she wasn't sure about their meaning here.

The last of the trees did not have any literature scribbled on its bark. Instead, she found a strange version of the letter M encased in a circle burned into the tree. Reaching out, she ran her fingers along the scorched bark, and in almost an instant, she felt sick. The sudden illness in her stomach caused her to take a step back before falling to her knees and retching up what was clearly the wine she had been sipping on last night.

Reaching for the tree to stable herself, Laura looked up to see her own hand come to land squarely in the middle of the M. An action that she tried to prevent but was either too weak or too late to stop.

Her head raced with images; flashes of people afire and smoke-filled villages filled her eyes, their screams muffled only by an even louder but harder-to-distinguish hissing sound. Her arm flared with pain, and she reared back, grasping at it. Holding her shoulder and clutching her arm to her chest, she grimaced. The pain, however, was the least of her worries.

Laura sat looking out onto the endless darkness that now surrounded her. "OK, Laura," she told herself. "Remain calm, and you can figure this out." She turned around slowly and with care, trying not to lose track of the direction that she had initially been facing.

Everything was black, and even the act of squinting produced no visual relief. For a moment, she began to wonder if she had gone blind. If touching that symbol could cause her to see and hear what wasn't there, then surely, it could have also blinded her.

Her breathing began to increase, and inside she started to sense a darkness tugging at her, claiming her. She could feel her arms grow cold, and the hair on them was undoubtedly standing on end. Her eyes began to tear up as she filled with fear. She knew this presence; it was the same as before; it was her haunter.

Suddenly, and as if it had never been, the darkness was gone, and she was now sitting on a plain of rugged terrain. The sky was gray and the ground barren of anything except for sharp boulders and the cracks in its surface. Standing, she slowly turned again, her concentration still on keeping her bearing.

At her left, she could see the silhouette of a mountain with dark clouds caressing its peak. Lightning as red as she had ever known flashed continuously, and once again, the pain in her arm flared to life. She grappled at it with her other hand, and then she heard the most terrifying thing she had ever heard.

"Lauraaaa." A voice that sounded so inhuman and yet so audible called her name. It hissed and gargled at her, the voice raspy but deep resembled that of the sound of sizzling meat, only it echoed with intensity.

In a state of panic, she spun around quickly, looking for any sign of an exit, and she found it. In front of her, in the distance, was the tree that had brought her here. She lunged forward with the intent of sprinting and reaching the tree, only to find that with each step she took she was no closer to her goal. She tried desperately to press on but as the fear that she would never reach the tree grew, her advance came to a halt, and Laura, with tear filled eyes, fell to her knees. When she landed, however, she wasn't face down, looking at the cracked earth of her previous surroundings.

Instead, she found herself back on her hands and knees facing a pile of red bile covering the red and cream Changpel rug beneath her chair.

Looking up, she was now sitting back in her apartment. The book she had been reading was neatly placed on the end table beside her, and the fire, while mostly ash, still smoldered from the top of a half-burned log that had toppled off to the side. Looking at the clock, Laura realized the time. "Damn," she muttered. She was late, very late…

* * *

The walk to the park was uneventful. The sky, its usual shade of gray for this time of year, was showing signs of a breach, and it was bitterly cold out. As I approached the entrance of J.A. Park, I noticed little in the way of anything I would have deemed as suspicious activity.

There were several parked cars here, but none of them were occupied. Outside its brick and iron gate, a woman seeking protection from the anticipated shower stood idly under a clear umbrella. She wore a blue denim jacket over a white-collared shirt, and her jeans were an odd shade of purple.

"Waiting on the bus," I said, shifting my attention to a couple of approaching joggers. They were dressed head to toe in skin-tight clothes, covered by a second layer that consisted of running shorts and matching marathon participant t-shirts. The couple quickly came and went. Looking around casually, I walked through the gate.

On the other side, I came to stand at the start of a trail that led directly into the center of a well-kept grove. Despite the bland nature of the sky, the park was teeming with vibrancy. All around, golden calendula flowers and bright pink snapdragons grew wildly in the fields of the park, and the trees as green as the moss at their feet formed a natural wall that seemingly enclosed the paradise.

The benches were empty this morning, a likely result of the approaching showers, and the only life to be found was that of the squirrels and birds. As I stepped out from the entrance and down the path a few feet, the smell of pine filled my nostrils immediately, and I couldn't help but smile.

Having grown up in the country, far away from the pungent smells that usually accompanied the city, I was well acquainted with this scent. And given that it wasn't too often that I got the chance just to stop and smell the trees, the nostalgia of the moment had been a welcomed distraction. "Hold it right there," a voice sounded from the tree line to my left. "No sudden movements," it said again. The distraction just became a little less welcomed.

Turning slowly, I came to face a very short and quite round man stepping out from behind the nearest tree. Had it not been for the snub-nosed .38 revolver that he had pointed at me, I wouldn't have even considered the man a threat. And even with the gun staring at me, there was nothing about him that made me nervous.

"I'm sorry. Who are you?" I asked, trying to keep calm so as not to wind up with a bullet in my belly.

"That's no concern of yours," he replied before pausing to pull a Zippo lighter from his pocket with his free hand and proceed to flip it fancily between his fingers and light it as it came to rest in his palm. He then lit the end of a fat Gordo cigar that already rested between his lips and extinguished the Zippo.

Judging from how far forward the cigar had been darkened by saliva, it had been there a while. "You know, chewing on those things is really bad for your lip."

He didn't take kindly to the comment. "Pipe it," he replied. My ensuing silence seemed to appease him, and he spoke again. "Good, now let's take a little walk." The man waved the front end of his gun in the direction of the tree line, and we began to walk down a narrow dirt path that was more of a trampled shortcut than anything else.

Marching deeper into the trees, the safety of the open area of the park began to fade from view. "Any particular place we're going?" I asked. My question clearly meant to annoy the man.

"Don't play stupid. You know what this is."

"Fair enough," I said, "but do I at least get to know why it is you want to kill me?"

"Let's just say you shouldn't have checked your mail this morning."

My mail, I thought to myself. *If this man was party to whoever kidnapped that woman and dropped off the letter, then he wouldn't be out here to kill me. That must mean he's trying to prevent me from meeting whoever sent that envelope. But why? Damn, I need to get more out of him.*

"OK, stop right there," he said abruptly.

Shit, there's no time. OK, Ray, my mind was racing. *He didn't bother to check you, and you know you're quick. All you have to do is turn around while pulling your gun from your shoulder holster, dive, and shoot. You've practiced this a hundred times, Ray. You've got this. OK, ready and g—*

My heart leaped at the sound of the gun going off behind me.

My hands raced to my chest, then frantically began feeling around the rest of my body. "I'm not shot," I mumbled while simultaneously checking myself. Satisfied that I had no new holes in me, I turned, drawing my .357 Colt Python, in exactly the fashion I had intended.

Only instead of seeing the short, fat cigar-smoking man that had walked me out here with the intent of killing me, I was now facing a lanky blond-haired man standing over his body, pistol in hand.

"Who the hell are you?" I said from my position on the ground.

"We don't have much time," he replied. "We have to go. I'll explain everything shortly."

I stood up, brushing the pine needles from my jacket the best I could. A gunshot in any other park might go unnoticed, but J.A. was one of the city's prides, and it probably wouldn't be too long before the police arrived. "Yeah," I said hesitantly before holstering my gun. "Lead the way."

Chapter 3

"No, Eddie," I said, "It wasn't the mailman—Look, when I grabbed the mail this morning, I found another unmarked, and when I opened it, I found these." Pulling the photographs from my jacket pocket, I tossed them on the table in front of me.

"It also came with a note suggesting that harm would come to the lady there if I didn't show up at the park." I pointed to the photograph of the woman as Eddie mulled it over. Laura sat staring intently at the other. "Is something the matter, Laura?" I asked.

"Oh, no, Ray, I'm fine." Her reply was hesitant. "It's just strange, is all. What is it?"

"Well, I'm not sure. From the looks of it, I'd say it's an amulet maybe or a coin of sorts, but what it's for, I don't know."

This wasn't true, of course. The thin man with blond hair had told me about the amulet and how it belonged to a man named Allister Bennings, the leader of a cult who claimed to be the overseers and protectors of evil.

The thought of anything evil needing protection didn't make any sense to me, but as the man put it, the cult kept a menagerie of what they considered to be misunderstood or misrepresented creatures, most of which were thought to be extinct and or to have never existed. He also warned me to take care of trusting anyone. And even though Laura and Eddie were perhaps the closest people to me, his warning was explicitly intended for those whom I might consider allies.

"There is none more efficient at bringing about the fall of a man than the betrayer with whom he shares his water." These were his exact words, and while there was no real reason to trust what he had told me, the fact that someone had tried to take my life that morning was enough for me to take the precaution of raising my guard a little.

"Who's the broad?" Eddie broke in as he took the photograph out from in front of Laura and exchanged it for the one in his hand.

"I don't know that either."

Eddie scoffed. "Why in the hell would someone send you a ransom note if it was someone you didn't know."

I sighed, and took a moment to consider my answer. "Again, I don't know. I didn't exactly get the chance to meet anyone who wasn't pointing a gun at me."

Another lie—well, sort of. The thin blond man, aka Lewis or so he claimed, may not have been pointing his gun at me with the intent of killing me, but it was still aimed in my direction after he shot the short, fat, cigar-smoking man.

The truth was that both men had intended to intercept me before I could meet with the parcel's sender. According to Lewis, the man was a well-known enforcer and member of the cult whose entire purpose for being in the park was to seek out and kill Ray Shields, i.e., me.

The connection here was that Lewis was also a member of the cult, and until recently, was a faithful member who truly believed that the cult's purpose was a righteous one. When I asked him what had changed, he looked me straight in the eye and said, "Nothing yet, but without you, everything will."

Of course, I had no idea what he was on about, but before I had the chance to ask him, he had started in on telling me who it was I was supposed to be meeting and why it was so important that he speak to me first. According to him, I was to be meeting a Miss Patricia Valentine, yet another cultist whose loyalties to the cult were in question.

Apparently, she and Lewis were working together to put a stop to whatever it was Mr. Bennings had planned. Still, Lewis said he was beginning to feel that Miss Valentine's methods were becoming too rash and unpredictable. "She is, after all, the reason you are being targeted," he had told me.

The pair had been devising a plan to slander Mr. Bennings and discredit him in front of the other members, but Patricia, whose intelligence is apparently rivaled only by her lack of impatience, had decided to enlist the help of a freelance reporter who, upon completing her part of the bargain and making public the fabricated evidence, was to be rewarded with an even bigger story.

Lewis, of course, knew she would never give up any of the cult's secrets and suspected that she planned to kill the reporter at the first available opportunity. She didn't, however, plan on the reporter doing any digging of her own and getting caught during one of the cult's fancy gatherings and leaving behind a trail of evidence that somehow implemented me as a possible threat to Benning's success. So much for being intelligent.

"Ray," Laura's voice broke my train of thought.

"How's that?" I said, clearly unaware of what I was being asked.

"You said they had a gun on you. How did you get yourself out of there? Do you think all this was just a ruse to get you alone so that someone could kill you?"

"Maybe," I replied, obviously lying again. "You know me, I always manage. I just waited for the right moment, and the guy got distracted."

The lie was now being built off my own carelessness which landed me in the situation in the first place. "We tussled, and he wound up running off when I dove for the gun he dropped."

"So, you have no idea who this fella was or what any of these pictures mean?"

I could tell by Eddie's voice that he wasn't buying it at all. "No, damn it." My voice carried with it the tone of annoyance, and while Laura may have chopped this up to me being frustrated at the lack of any answers, Eddie knew me better and undoubtedly understood that I was tired of making excuses.

"Laura, you look a bit tired," he said, clearly attempting to bring an end to her being part of the conversation.

"Well, I suppose I am. I didn't sleep well last night and—Oh!" She jumped at the recollection of her failure to show up for work this morning. "Ray, I'm sorry I didn't make it in to work today. I may have had a little too much wine last night, and I suppose that coupled with the rough night's sleep, caused me to just sleep through the day."

"Don't worry about it," I replied, "If you had been at the office, you would have checked the mail yourself, and I wouldn't have been able to keep you from coming to the park with me."

I looked up long enough to wave down the waitress with the notion that I wanted my bill and looked back at Laura and Eddie. "Why don't you head back home and try to get a good night's rest this time? After all, without you at the office to make the morning brew, everything seems to go awry."

Laura smiled. "All right, Ray," she replied. "But only because you asked so nicely." She stood straightening the wrinkles from her jacket, took another glance at the pictures on the table, said goodbye to Eddie, nodded to me, and made her way to the front of the diner.

Eddie and I watched in silence as Laura walked to her car. Her steps were almost unearthly, and what gentlemen that Eddie and I may or may not have been, we never passed up the opportunity to watch Laura come and go. "She sure is something else, ain't she?" Eddie said calmly before changing back to his regular tough-guy self.

"Yea, I suppose so," I agreed, pulling a few dollars out of my billfold to pay the waitress who had returned while Eddie and I were mesmerized at our colleague's exit.

"I gotta go." I looked at Eddie for a moment, trying to decide whether or not to share what I had chosen to hide 'til now or to let it be until I knew for sure my closest comrade wasn't playing on the opposite team. I decided to play it safe.

"I'll see you back at the office. I have something I want to look into first."

Eddie sat quietly, his gaze still out the window. "Whatever you say, boss," he gibed with perfect timing as I turned and headed for the door.

Chapter 4

Eddie watched Ray make his way out of the diner and across the street before getting up to follow him. The two men had worked together for nearly fifteen years, and in all that time, he had never known Ray to keep something from him.

That alone was reason enough for him to tail Ray. Besides, whatever he was hiding must be bad if he would lie to Eddie about it. Eddie hated liars, and Ray knew that better than anyone. It was, after all, the sole reason that he stuck to asking questions around bars and let Ray handle all the interviews that took place in a more professional setting.

In the bar, Eddie knew how to get someone talking. Drink as much as they do, and they trust you won't remember, that or they just see another drunk whose problems couldn't possibly be as bad as theirs and, in keeping with the psychology of man, proceeded to see who had outdone the other.

Whatever the case, in the bar, few people lied to Eddie, and when someone did manage to keep their wits about them, the resulting brawl that generally ensued could easily be chalked up to a couple of drunks having a disagreement.

Leaving the diner, Eddie crossed the street a little further down so that he could be sure that Ray didn't stop around the corner to watch and see if his partner was going to follow him. He hadn't; Another sign that told Eddie whatever it was that Ray was hiding was serious. Ray, being as sharp as he was, must have known that Eddie didn't buy into his lies, and he was either too occupied with thinking about what it was he had to do, or he was too busy to care.

He walked for nearly ten minutes before catching sight of the tail end of Ray's jacket just as he rounded another corner. He didn't need to keep Ray in sight to follow him.

Aside from being pretty sure where Ray was heading, Eddie was no newbie to the art of cat and mouse and was, according to Ray, the best there was. He had once tailed a burglar from the scene of the crime all the way across the city without eyes on the thief for a good hour and a half.

His secret was to pay attention to everyone but the man he was stalking. People, regardless of their own agenda, have a habit of watching others go about their daily lives. The key, as Eddie put it, was to look for those who were not actively engaged in their own happenings, in order to determine who might have spotted someone who, for one reason or another, stood out to them.

As was the case with the burglar, those who are trying to hide generally stand out, and as such, all Eddie had to do was follow the trail of glances and intrigued stares. In Ray's case, that jacket of his and his determined walk were enough for anyone he passed to stop and wonder what this fella might be up to.

And though the rain on this particular evening had most people staying indoors, Eddie still managed to track his partner off the few street hooligans that braved the rain in search of mischief.

At the corner of twelfth and Smith, Eddie watched Ray stop out in front of the park and take notice of a woman who stood under an umbrella by the gate. Shaking his head, he walked directly up to her and began to exchange a few words.

Eddie watched the conversation with curiosity. There was nothing particularly interesting about this woman. Aside from the clear umbrella that she hid under, he would have guessed she was simply another person with the unfortunate luck of having to work long hours on this gloomy day and was now waiting to catch her bus home.

Then again, Ray must have had a reason. The hasty retreat from the diner and the fact that he headed directly back to the park told Eddie that whoever it was that Ray was speaking to now must be tied into this morning's happenings somehow.

After a few minutes, Ray turned away from the woman and headed into the park. The woman turned and headed in the opposite direction. As much as he wanted to speak to the woman himself, Eddie knew that Ray would come clean once he confronted him, so he opted for keeping his tail on Ray and headed into the park.

Inside, Eddie watched as Ray walked over to a bench in the center of the clearing. The bench was dark brown with black iron rails and matched every other bench in the park. The only thing special about it was that this one had a mess of discarded newspapers on it that were now dampened by the rain and practically melting through the slats.

It wasn't the newspapers that interested Ray, though, it was what they hid. Eddie figured they were covering some kind of correspondence left by the lady at the front of the park, and now, as Ray dove his hand into the slosh and pulled out a dark yellow envelope, his suspicions were confirmed.

After giving Ray a moment to look through the contents, he decided it was time to confront his partner, so he stepped out from under the cover of the park's gated arches and made his way over to him.

* * *

"Ugh," I groaned in annoyance. Not only had I completely misread the woman who had been standing outside of the park this morning, but I now had a sleeve covered in what appeared to be a mash-up of the Sunday funnies and the 'your horoscope' section of today's newspaper.

"Figures," I said to myself, shaking loose the last of my newly acquired attire. The envelope was identical to the one I had received at my office and, even though this one was wet and likely to lose its integrity once it was opened, it also carried the same scent.

Stepping out of the rain and under the cover of a tree next to the bench, I tore open the envelope and emptied its contents into my hand. I wasn't surprised to see that it contained another photograph of the bound reporter, though I did half expect to see her in a different state.

Fortunately, she didn't appear to be any worse off than before, but she certainly had a more fearful look in her eyes. The only other thing in the envelope was a map with a circle drawn on it and the words Le Chateau written in red.

"What have you got there, Ray?" I sighed at the sound of Eddie's voice and looked up to see him joining me under the tree. His hands were in his pockets, and he wore a dour expression on his face.

"Another piece to the puzzle," I said, locking eyes with him.

"All right then, spill it. Who was that lady out front, and why were you lying back at the diner?"

Both were valid questions, and though I still had my reservations, I figured that trusting Eddie was better than going it alone, that, and I knew he wouldn't just let it go.

"She's—" I paused "—not who I was expecting. And as for the diner—Well, I lied because I don't know enough about what's going on to know who to trust."

Eddie's eyebrow raised in protest to the comment. "Look, I lied about not meeting anyone else this morning. The man with the gun who tried to kill me was shot shortly after walking me out into those trees." I paused and nodded in the direction of the tree line behind Eddie. "The man who killed him had a great deal of information to share with me, including a warning of caution in trusting anyone, especially those closest to me. Until I knew more, I didn't want to take the risk."

Eddie stood silently for a moment, and I was beginning to wonder if he was considering whether or not he wanted to accept my explanation or if he just wanted to make me feel uncomfortable for lying to him. His expression relaxed, and he shrugged. "Eh, I guess I would have done the same." He took a few steps closer and took the map from my hand. "So, what did this other guy tell you exactly?"

Eddie and I stood under the tree in the park, and I shared with him the details of my morning. I recounted the walk to the park and my incorrect analysis of the woman out front.

Apparently, he had made the same assumption. I briefly described the fat cigar-smoking man. Then told him about Lewis and Miss Valentine, their connection to a cult run by a man named Allister Bennings, and his desire to use the amulet from the photograph to un-imprison something that Lewis referred to only as the Cherufe.

It was a lot to share, and though I tried not to leave anything out, Eddie made sure to question my story where anything seemed to be missing. He was particularly interested in the reporter for some reason, but he just said it was because he hated seeing a damsel in distress. He then went on to remind me of my encounter with Laura and how I took on her case free of charge. He had me there.

By the end of our conversation, it was nearing eleven, and at Eddie's suggestion, we resolved to meet at the office in the morning before heading out to the location circled on the map and to let Laura know we were going to be gone for most of the day investigating the B. Dalton case.

He wasn't initially on board with leaving Laura in the dark, but when I reminded him of the warning and noted that if there were any legitimacy to it, and if he was confident that he could be trusted, then Laura would be the only person that that warning could apply to, he agreed to keep everything between us for now.

Chapter 5

Aside from catching a flat a mile or two from our destination, everything that morning went off without a hitch. Laura made it to work and had a cup of coffee waiting for me when I arrived and Eddie, in what must have been a gesture of pity for keeping Laura in the dark, actually bothered to have his jacket dry-cleaned and was sporting it around haughtily. Where he found the time to do this, I couldn't say, but given the length of time we just spent together in the car, I was thankful.

"Rotten luck with that tire, boss," he remarked. His newly cleaned jacket now hung over his shoulder as we made our way down a dirt road, and looking at him, he almost seemed like a different person. "Yeah, I suppose."

We had only just turned off the main road a few miles from where the tire blew, but walking back to it wouldn't have done us any good. Of the five hours driving, the last hour had been spent winding down a tiny two-lane mountain pass surrounded by forest. We hadn't seen a single car in all that time, so the likelihood of us catching one anytime soon was slim.

There wasn't much to the dirt road. Hell, it wasn't even on the map. Had Eddie not spotted the drive just as we passed by, I'm certain we would have wound up driving all the way up the mountain.

"Could be worse, though," he said, breaking the silence between us again. I could tell Eddie was phishing for a conversation, and though he was right in that our walk had been mostly shaded with spurts of sunlight beaming through the trees and was accompanied by the peaceful chirping of the forest's residents, I too was beginning to feel the need of conversation. The drive had been long and silent. My own fault really, as I tend to focus on the road and retreat into my own head.

"Yeah, we could be spending the time preparing for another court appearance," I said. Eddie Scoffed at the comment. As much as we enjoyed our work, sitting in courtrooms waiting to testify was our least favorite part of the job.

"Say, Ray, what do you suppose this place looks like?"

"I'm not sure, but if it's way out here, it's either falling apart or—" I trailed off just as we topped a slope in the road and came to face what was with all certainty, our destination.

Eddie and I looked at each other for a moment, then back to the small castle in front of us. The writing on the map said Le Chateau, so it was only natural to assume that we would wind up standing at the door to a home of wealth, but this exceeded any expectation we may have had.

The architecture was astonishing, and its neo-gothic design was so well executed that I nearly forgot where and when I was. The building was a towering four stories with several vaulted ceilings, high arches, and rising turrets attached to the front.

But, as deserving as it was to be noted for its perfect design, this place exuded terror as much as it evoked fascination. Ivy, the colors of dark green and a deep red, covered vast portions of the wall, and judging from the extent of its growth, it likely did the same all the way around the building.

"Sheesh. You would think that someone who could afford a place like this could also afford to have the windows cleaned." Eddie's observation of the unattended windows only added to the creepy vibe I was beginning to get.

"Yeah," I said, agreeing with him before suggesting we take a closer look.

As we approached what had to be the main entrance, I noted the presence of the same strange symbol from the photograph carved into the stone just above the door. It looked no different from in the picture, but seeing it set in stone like it was, and in person, really added to the discomfort that I felt about the whole situation.

I was just about to reach for the heavy iron knocker when Eddie stopped me. "Why bother?" he said. "We were pretty much invited. We might as well make ourselves at home." And with that, he reached for the latch and opened the door.

As thick as it was, a clear sign of its weight, and with the lack of attention to the windows, I expected the door to let out a loud creaking sound when Eddie pushed it open. There was nothing. Eddie looked over his shoulder, and I could tell that he had been expecting it to render the same effect, and he was clearly as surprised as I was that it didn't.

He shrugged and stepped inside. I looked around, taking in the glory of the chateau's magnificent exterior one last time before following my partner inside.

While the outside of this manor suggested the place had been abandoned, the meticulous care of everything on its interior suggested quite the opposite. Recently polished white marble floors greeted us as we entered, and numerous paintings, all in their gilded frames, hung evenly and appeared to be well cared for.

At the center of the foyer, an imperial staircase with a wide base that narrowed just under a large archway before splitting in two directions led to a second floor. It was carpeted with a navy-blue rug adorned with gold printed Fleur de Lys that complimented the manor's gray stone walls. As far as appearances go, this looked like the home of a very well-off and very strict individual, at least in terms of cleanliness.

One thing did seem out of place, though. There appeared to be an uneven count of statues in the room. Rather, one seemed to be missing. Aside from the evenly distributed marble heads that were set atop wooden pedestals on both sides of the staircase, both banisters were complete with square pillars that, judging from the one on the left, should have been topped with a gargoyle guardian.

The lone gargoyle stood about two feet tall, shoulders back, chest out, and wings slightly raised. Its proud posture was accompanied by a very muscular physique, and regardless of being made from stone, it had a very sturdy appearance.

"This thing looks almost like a small man," I said, realizing I was speaking to myself only when I looked up to see Eddie making his way over to a bookshelf on the left side of the staircase.

What was most intriguing about the life-like gargoyle was how its tail, which extended another two feet from its body, wrapped around the banister and wove between two of the legs. The tail didn't appear to be made into the banister, and yet it was wrapped so tightly around the legs that I couldn't fathom how it had been placed.

"Say, Eddie, maybe don't touch anything. This stuff looks really expensive," I said, recalling a time when Eddie once knocked over an unfinished painting in the hall of an artist client of ours. The arrangement that followed the incident cost us both two months' pay. He gave no response, but I was sure he heard me.

I made my way over to the wall of paintings with my hands behind my back. I began eyeing them as if I were walking through a gallery of fine art, stopping only briefly to give them each a once-over before moving on to the next piece to be analyzed.

I was about to walk away when I stopped in front of a painting that captured my attention wholly. It was of medial size, just a tad bigger than your average eight-and-a-half by eleven-inch notepad, and bore a slightly more tarnished frame than the others. It was by no means an extravagant work of art. In fact, it paled in comparison to the lavish works that surrounded it, and still, it was somehow the focal point of my attention.

In the center of the painting sat a balloon salesman hunched over on a small and seemingly old wooden stool. His face lacked any real expression, save for a slight upward curve to the side of his lip, and he was otherwise very plainly present, dressed in a light brown long coat with matching pants.

His pushcart, on the other hand, anchor to the fifty or so realistically painted balloons that shaded him from the sun, appears to capture the attention of a young boy, whose fascination with the colorful cloud has him attempting to break free of his mother's grasp.

"Excuse me, gentlemen, can I help you?" Eddie and I turned to see a tall woman enter the foyer from a room to our right. She was taller than both of us, had long black hair, and wore a fiery red and orange pendant around her neck. The jewel was stunning but didn't match well with the grayish-green cardigan that she was wearing. Had it not been for the black and silver buttons, the entire outfit might have been a wash.

"Ray Shields," I said, thrusting my hand out in introduction. She took my hand in hers, and I could tell by the look on her face this was not the first time she had heard the name. She must have realized that she was in danger of giving away that secret, because she relaxed her expression quickly and smiled. "Pleasure," she said, shifting her attention over to Eddie as he fumbled to put a book back on the shelf. "And you are?"

"Oh err," he managed to re-shelve the volume quickly enough to not look like a complete klutz, though judging from her glance at the shelf, he definitely misplaced it. "Eddie," he responded simply, bringing his hand out in front of him and then back to his side after realizing he was standing a good ten feet away from her.

There was no recovering from that. "Do you have an interest in philosophy, Mr. Eddie?" she said as she walked over to the shelf and removed the volume, only to place it a good three books over.

"Ha," I let out an unexpected laugh that caused Eddie and our new host to turn their heads in my direction.

The laugh was involuntary, of course, but the thought of Eddie reading a book that endeavored to analyze man's behavior put a far too amusing image in my head. He had enough trouble as it was holding his tongue when people expressed their personal views back at the office, so naturally, the picture that played over in my head was of Eddie knocking back a flask on page two of Martin Heidegger's Being and Time.

"Sorry," I said, circling back to answer her first question. "Look, Miss—" I stopped, realizing she hadn't given me her name, and then stood there waiting for her to do so. When it was clear that she had no intention of telling it to me, I continued. "We would like to speak with Mr. Bennings if that's possible. We're investigating the disappearance of a reporter by the name of Emily Garcia. She went missing a little over a week ago, and we have reason to believe that she met with Mr. Bennings sometime before her disappearance."

"I see," she said, pausing briefly to caress the spine of another book with her index finger. "Mr. Bennings is currently unavailable." She turned and walked back toward the center of the foyer, "But if you don't mind waiting, I can see about freeing him up."

I nodded in agreement, and she beckoned for us to follow her. So, we did.

She led us back through the room that she had used to enter the foyer, and I was shocked to see that it was barren of any decorations except for what appeared to be an enlarged bear head hanging above a rather impressive fireplace on the other side of the room. The room was empty, besides this curiosity, a side table, and two armchairs that set atop a massive fur rug.

"Is that a trophy?" I said, gesturing in the direction of the wall mount and what was, in all likelihood, its other half.

"No, that is Onikumu," she said, coming to an abrupt halt before turning to face the both of us. "Please have a seat while I sort out a brief meeting for you with Mr. Bennings."

Without waiting for a response, she quickly turned and left us standing alone.

Eddie and I probably wouldn't have taken a seat had it not been for the lack of decorum. Sitting allowed us both to get a closer look at the bear's head and fur, and since there was nothing else to look at, neither of us hesitated. "I've never seen a bear up close, but this is definitely bigger than I imagined."

Eddie's remark sank in as he sunk into the chair. He wasn't wrong, the head was twice the size of even the largest Kodiak, and if the fur was, in fact, the rest of it, then this bear would have been the size of your average sedan. "No kidding." My amazement was as apparent as his.

"What do you think of our host?" I asked, curious to see if he would give a flustered response.

"Well, she certainly is pretty, but I don't think she likes me much."

"That's probably because you don't share the same passion for philosophy," I said, jokingly referring to his misplacement of the book.

"Yeah, yeah, at least she didn't get all sour when I told her my name." His retort was as accurate as my own jab. "You caught that too, eh?"

We must have sat there for nearly ten minutes, just long enough for our interest in the bear to fade before Eddie's patience wore off. "Screw this," he said, rising to his feet. "I say we go find this Bennings's character on our own."

I would have been inclined to disagree had I not been curious about the rest of the mansion. "Fine," I said. "But try not to touch anything this time." I could tell by the way he was strolling off in the direction that our host left that he was smiling and that my request was unlikely to be granted.

The poorly lit hallway that we entered led us through another two rooms, more closely resembling the main foyer than the room we were left to sit in. It then opened up into a kitchen that looked like it was meant to prepare food for groups much larger than your average family. Three large brick ovens lined the wall to our left.

An island the size of the bearskin sat in the middle of the room with racks upon racks of pots and pans and other assorted kitchenware hanging chaotically above it, and there were so many cabinets and drawers and bins that I decided against the idea of counting them. In the corner of the room, there was an arched doorway that led to a stairwell, which, from my current angle, appeared to go both up and down.

We stopped here and took a moment to consider carrying on into the next room or taking the stairs up when Eddie and I both froze at the sound of a loud screech that came from behind us.

"What the hell was that?" I said, reaching for my shoulder-holstered Colt Python.

"I don't know, but I sure as hell don't want to find out." Eddie pulled free his own 38 Detective Special and made it ready for use.

"Better to face it head-on than to get chased down," I said, taking a step back toward the hall. The screech came again, only this time it was much closer, and as Eddie and I turn toward it, I caught a glimpse of something moving quickly toward us from down the hall.

"Eddie!" I yelled, spinning back just in time to fire a single round that missed my attacker before being hit dead-on by the shoulder of what looked like the world's largest, meatiest, most muscular Mastiff. I was tossed across the island, taking with me about half the kitchenware. The wind entirely knocked out of me and my gun, God knows where; I reached for the first thing I could grab while simultaneously trying to stand up.

Two more gunshots erupted from in front of me before Eddie too came flying across the island, taking with him most of the remaining items from the racks. I got to my feet, but there was another flash, and I was struck hard by the creature's colossal paw, again throwing me across the room. I'm not sure which hurt more, being plowed into, thrown into the racks and pelted with falling pots, or being swatted full force into the wall of ovens, with a gash being left in my side.

I glanced at Eddie, hoping that he managed to stay armed. He hadn't. He was in the same predicament that I was. "Shit," I managed to gasp, rolling out of the way of more flying debris.

"Grrraahhh—" The beast let out a huge cry, rearing back to stand on its hind legs. This was no Mastiff. It was like nothing I've ever seen. It towered over Eddie, standing nearly ten feet tall, and its muscles were unbelievable.

Eddie fumbled to stand as the creature brought its head back down, and I knew I had to find a way to get us out of here, or this was the end of us. The hall was out of the question, and the beast was in front of the other entrance. Whatever we did, the stairs were our only option for escape.

Finally, making it to his feet, Eddie was able to get his hands on a rolling pin just as the beast came bearing down on him. He jammed the pin into its mouth, saving his head from becoming its dinner. Scrambling to help Eddie, I tossed a sizable four-slice toaster, being the closest thing in my reach. It hit but rendered no effect.

On my second try, I paid more attention to my choice of weapons, managing to get my hands on a hefty cast-iron skillet. From my now kneeling position, I drew back and let it fly with all my might, landing a solid hit to the side of the creature's face. It let out a hissing yelp and leaped back, freeing Eddie before turning its attention to me.

"THE STAIRS!" I yelled as loudly as possible. Eddie, no longer the target, was able to make a run for his gun. In a state of near panic, I picked up a log from the pile of lumber used to heat the stoves, and in doing so, I uncovered a small axe.

When I looked back at the creature, I could see that it was fully aware of my newly found weapon, and it had no intention of giving me long enough to grab it. Just then, Eddie fired a barrage of bullets at the creature. It wasn't enough to put it down, but it gave me the time I needed to toss the log, grab the axe, rear it back, and strike just as the beast lunged at me.

"Grrahh—gh—" The creature reared back, swiping its massive paw wildly, and for the third time, tossed me across the room. The axe was ripped free from my grasp, but my swing had been true. The axe was planted firmly into its neck, and it couldn't even let out a proper growl. Meaning I must have hit its vocal box.

The beast brought its eyes down to face me. It stared at me with the purest hate, and its chest began to glow a deep red, then it lunged forward again. As I got to my feet, Eddie grabbed hold of my collar and yanked, pulling us into the stairwell just before it reached me and suddenly exploded into a ball of fire that ripped the two of us apart, thrusting me up the stairs and him down them.

All the being tossed around took its toll on my ability to tell up from down, so, at that moment, I could only assume that was the direction I was tossed. While rotating in the air, I finally came to face a partially opened door, giving me just enough time to raise my hands not a moment before impact.

* * *

I don't know how long I had been out, but judging from the still-floating particles of ash, I assumed it had only been a matter of minutes. My ears were ringing something fierce, and I was in all kinds of pain, but I knew I couldn't afford to sit still and attempt a recovery. The four-claw gash in my side had drenched my shirt, and it was clear from the amount of blood on the floor that I would need to dress the wound quickly, or I wasn't going to be conscious much longer.

I dragged myself to a sitting position against the wall and haphazardly let my head fall to the left and then to the right attempting to locate anything that I could use to stop the bleeding and, as a byproduct of that action, get some kind of bearings about me.

I was sitting at the end of another hallway. To my left was a large, heavily draped window that barely let in enough light for me to see that the other direction was empty of life and of anything I could use as a dressing. I thought of cutting the drapes, but when I realized I didn't have the means to do so, I gave up on the idea of dressing the wound.

Instead, I turned my attention to the wooden door through which I had been thrust through. It was as charred as I was but not nearly as lucky. I located a nearby piece that was still smoldering, and after using what little breath I had in me to blow on it and ensure it was well embered, I put it to my chest.

The next few minutes were a cross between pain and numbness, accompanied by cries of agony and grunts of motivation. Each time I pressed the ember to my chest, it felt like every exposed piece of skin was being torn again and again, and every time I took it away, the relief that I felt was almost euphoric. Had it not been for the smell of burning flesh and the sizzle of the blood and skin, I would have forgotten the initial pain altogether.

Eventually, the deepest gash had been sealed, and I was able to stop the unpleasant act of self-treatment and was, at last, able to lay my head back against the wall and recover.

In doing so, I thought first of Laura, wondering how she would take the news if Eddie got out of here and I didn't.

Then, after thinking about Eddie, my mind began to wonder if he was even still alive. He had been behind me when the beast exploded, but he was also tossed down the stairs and therefore not only suffered the concussion of the explosion but was also at the mercy of gravity. I reassured myself that he was ok. It was Eddie I was talking about, after all. And then I passed out for a second time.

The next time I opened my eyes, I was no longer propped up against the wall by a smoldering pile of monster and doorframe. Instead, I found myself lying on an antique couch in a small room. If I had to guess by the size of the room, I would say it was a servant's quarter, but the furniture there suggested otherwise.

"Oh good, you're awake." For the briefest moment, I thought I was thinking out loud, then as my brain's deductive functioning began to kick back in, I realized it wasn't my voice I was hearing. I set myself up and let my eyes focus as Lewis came into view. "That was quite a ruckus you caused, Ray. Do you have any idea how lucky you are to be alive right now?"

"Tell me about it," I grunted, my annoyance at his comment being made clear.

"You're lucky I found you before anyone else did."

I wasn't too sure what he meant by anyone else. The fact that Eddie and I hadn't seen anyone other than that tall, mysterious woman with zero sense of fashion had me questioning the legitimacy of this so-called cult.

According to Eddie, for a cult to truly be a cult, it had to have two things: one a leader skilled in the art of coercion and deceit, and two, a flock of gullible guppies who are willing to be persuaded into believing in a false reality, all in exchange for not having to toil with the demands of the real world.

Eddie's pastime of reading tabloid conspiracies didn't make him an expert, but it was a common-sense argument. Then again, there was that creature that tried to kill us, an event that was making it extremely hard to conclude that this was just your ordinary con.

"Who was that woman with all the good looks but no taste? And what the hell was that thing? And how did you even know I was here?" Lewis stared at me for a moment in what I assumed was his trying to prioritize my questions.

"That was Valora. She interrupted Magister Bennings at our morning gathering. When I saw her make a hasty exit after being scolded in front of the others for her interruption, I thought it might be a good idea to follow her and see what was going on."

"And the beast?" I asked.

"I think you misunderstand Ray. They are… um were… one and the same."

"Wait, what?" I was staring at him in complete confusion.

"Valora was a Cynanthrope. A Dog Woman. She heralded from the Molossian breed of ancient Greece. Sadly, she was the last of her kind."

"I'm sorry, but you're telling me that that beast, that thing that tried to kill Eddie and me, is, or was, really a woman."

"Yes, Ray, that's what I'm telling you. I know it's hard to believe, but it's true. Valora was the one who greeted you and the one who tried to kill you."

I wasn't sure if I believed what he was telling me, but I decided it was easier to play along than it was to sort everything out at the immediate moment.

"OK, say I believe you. Why is it that you feel sorry for her?"

"Don't mistake my desire to see Mr. Bennings removed from his position as magister as a complete change in my beliefs, Ray, I still very much believe in what we stand for here. And Valora was—" He trailed off for a moment, appearing to try and collect himself. He seemed wounded at the loss of Valora, and I was beginning to regret my remark.

"She was the guardian of this house and its flock. A creature of genuine strength worthy of the title she held as the champion of Thessaly."

"Thess—agh," I groaned in my attempt to stand while also trying to clarify what he said. "Did you just say Thessaly?"

"Yes, Ray. I did. She was one of the few Cynanthropes to survive that war, and now, thanks to you, she is gone."

"Look, I don't mean to offend you, Lewis, but you can't expect me to be all broken up about what happened. I remind you, she tried to kill me."

"Yes, Ray, she did, and it's precisely the kind of poor leadership that led to that unfortunate incident that drives me to see Magister Bennings removed from his position. Valora—her breed is—was, loyal above all else and today she proved her loyalty one final time when she attempted to kill you, Ray Shields, the man who is a threat to her master's success."

OK, now I did feel bad for killing her, but what did he mean by me being a threat to Bennings's success? This was the second time he let on to my having a role in all of this, and I intended to find out what that role was.

"What does that mean, Lewis?" I asked, making sure to look him directly in the eye when I did.

"There isn't time for me to explain that to you right now. While you were unconscious, I went back to where you and Valora fought, only to find that the magister and the others had already arrived. He was yelling at them that he wanted you and your partner found. Can I assume you didn't come alone then?"

"No, my partner Eddie—" I paused, recalling the moment the explosion ripped us apart.

"He was blown down the stairs when it happened, and obviously, I don't know what happened to him."

"Right, well, everyone is looking for the both of you, and it's only a matter of time before they find you. Here," he pulled my gun out from under his cloak and handed it to me. "I found it lying under a pile of logs in the kitchen. Try not to kill any more of my friends, Ray."

It was odd that I hadn't noticed the outfit he was wearing until just now, but at the jabbing reminder that I killed someone or something that he had some manner of respect for, I withheld making any comment about the ridiculous cloak.

"Yeah, I'll do my best," I said, very uncertain of how one responds to a demand like that. "One question, though," I continued as I stood up, grimacing at the pain in the side of my abdomen. "If everyone is looking for me, how are we going to find Eddie?"

"Not we, you, and that's going to be easier than you think."

He walked to the other side of the room and took a book from the shelf on the wall. He removed a small key that had been placed inside of it and walked back over to me. "You'll need this," he said, handing it to me. He then walked around to the back of the couch and, with a swipe of his foot, pushed the rear leg underneath it.

Hearing a slight clicking sound, I looked up to see a crease appear on the wall behind him. "This place has a number of passages that can be used to get around, and since only a few of us know about them and no one is expecting you to, it should be safe for you to move about them."

"What about you?" I asked. "I'll be making sure to keep everyone otherwise occupied with looking in all the wrong places. Now, just go down the passage, and when you get to the next wall, you will see a set of stairs that lead down. I'm sure you'll find your friend down there somewhere."

I wasn't entirely satisfied with the answer he had given me, and though I wanted to prod him more, I knew I needed to find Eddie and get out of here.

"One more thing, Ray, that key will open the cell holding the woman you came for. You need to get her out of here, and when you do, I promise you'll have all the answers you can take."

With that, he closed the passage door, and I could hear him make his way out of the small room. I turned and made my way down yet another very poorly lit hallway.

Unable to shake off the shock of what had just taken place, Eddie reached into his jacket for the tin of jack he had just filled this morning. His hand came to rest on it, and he realized the area around the pocket was wet and that the tin was all bent out of shape and no longer sealed its contents inside. "So much for keeping Laura off my back," he said as he let the last drop tickle his tongue.

Eddie continued down the hallway, taking special care to stop at each door and give his attention to the strange images on them.

Eventually, he came to stand in front of a door that was slightly ajar and bore the image of a horrifyingly large beast resembling a war dog of the ancient Greeks, only with half its chest peeled away with what appeared to be a burning ball of fire where the heart should be. "That must be our friend from earlier," he mumbled to himself as he checked the dressing that covered the gash in his arm.

During the deadly encounter upstairs, he had managed to remain unharmed all the way until the final moments when the beast that attacked him and Ray exploded. He had seen the look in its eyes after Ray stuck an axe into its neck, and when it began to glow, he had a split-second recollection of reading about a demon creature that exploded after being captured by the Chinese military.

The article had made mention of reports by survivors seeing the creature's chest glowing red just before it went boom. Obviously, he hadn't believed a word of it then, but at that moment, when their attacker reared back, and its chest began to glow, he just knew what was coming.

The ensuing explosion and the concussions that sent Ray up the stairs and him down them also completely destroyed the stairwell. This not only made it impossible to get back up to his partner, but it also sent enough debris flying through the air that Eddie was sure he was lucky to have only been hit in the arm.

He retrieved his pistol from its holster and peered inside the door. He was surprised to see the room was a small, well-kept bedroom complete with a small writing desk, a bed, and an amour decorated with intricate carvings of men and women walking through what seemed to be an endless field.

Hesitating to trust his own eyes, he pushed the door entirely open only to jump at the surprisingly loud scraping sound that it made as it swung awkwardly on the hinges dragging a torn corner against the floor. He paused, stood in silence for a moment, looked back down the hallway to make sure no one was coming, and then entered the room.

There was nothing special about the bed. It was a twin-sized mattress with black sheets and a single pillow; nothing more. It took a moment for him to open the amour as it was locked, but it was just a piece of furniture, so it wasn't too hard to pry open.

Once inside, he noted that none of the clothing really matched or looked like they would even remotely go well with each other. This made him wonder if all cultists had bad taste in clothing.

Eddie turned his attention to the desk and walked back to the front of the room, where he picked up a journal that was sitting there. It was leather-bound, brown, and had the letter V crudely scraped into the cover.

When he opened it, he found a single picture of a woman and a child of about six, standing in front of a modest little house with the silhouette of some mountains in the background. The picture was old and therefore not very clear, but he couldn't help but think that he knew this woman. He held the picture closer, and as he strained his eyes to get a better look at her, it hit him.

The clothes, the black hair, and the height of the woman in the photograph. This was the lady from the entrance, the one who greeted him and Ray. But why would her room be down here, and why would it be in a hall filled with rooms that he had first assumed might contain the creatures that were represented by the placards on the front of them?

As he looked back at the picture, he noticed a small but bright glow near her neckline. "The necklace," he said, looking up as if everything made sense and at the same time didn't.

Eddie stuffed the journal into his jacket pocket, replacing the tin of Jack that he tossed earlier, and hastily stepped out of the room and around to the front of the door to look at the placard on it. "It can't be," he said to himself.

The necklace, this placard, the deep glow in the beast's chest. It didn't make any logical sense, and yet somehow, it made all the sense in the world.

As Eddie stood there trying to wrap his head around the current mystery, he heard something coming from further down the hallway. When he turned, he saw what looked like a small man standing there staring at him. It was a long hallway, and it was dark, so he couldn't be sure, but it definitely looked like the little man had wings.

"Scraaac," the figure made a screeching sound, and though it was much quieter, Eddie realized it was the same sound that he and Ray had heard earlier, just before being attacked.

Given the level of danger this place has already presented, he thought about raising his gun, but he didn't. Instead, he stood there looking at the small figure, watching it intently, waiting to see what it was going to do.

"Scraaac." It sounded off for a second time and then slowly raised its arm and pointed off to its left. Eddie continued to study the figure. It was definitely shaped like a small man, but when it raised its arm in what looked like an attempt to give directions, Eddie was able to confirm the existence of what he earlier thought to be wings.

"OK, now that's not normal," he said quietly. Neither was the size and shape of the little man, but at least that was closer to real for him than a man with wings.

The figure stood perfectly still, staring back at Eddie, its left arm still extended away from its body. Then, in a flash, it leaped up to the ceiling, spinning skillfully, and planted itself firmly against the concrete above. Then, with one quick glance back at Eddie, it scurried off in the direction it had been pointing. Eddie was shocked by the agility that the figure had shown, and he was now one hundred percent sure that this thing was not a man. What it was, he didn't know, but it wasn't human.

Deciding it was best to not linger, he started making his way after the winged creature. Whatever it was, it didn't attack him, and judging from its action, it may have actually been trying to help him.

Eddie moved with haste, but he did not run. The last thing he wanted to do was turn a corner and come face to face with something else that wanted to kill him. When he arrived at the first turn, he peered down the hall and saw the little figure was waiting at the other end, still effortlessly clinging to the ceiling. As he began making his way down the second hall, the figure turned and scurried off again.

Eddie continued to follow it cautiously and made sure to pay attention to the doors he passed and the turns he made, lest he get turned around in pursuit of the creature, becoming unable to find his way back if the need be.

After a few twists and turns, Eddie stopped short of another corner when he heard a shrill cry from the other end. It was a woman's scream, though it didn't seem to carry the sound of terror. Instead, it sounded like a determined battle cry. Eddie raised his pistol and turned the corner.

At the end of the hall, the creature he had been following stood firm under a lamp facing the yells that were now clearly directed at him. He was entirely visible, and Eddie had to take a few more cautious steps forward to make sure that he wasn't seeing things. The creature's skin was a pale green, almost like that of a toad only smooth, and it stood well built, approximately three feet tall, and had a tail that was a little over half the size of its body and about as thick as its arm.

"I'll be damned," he said. He didn't bother keeping his voice down this time, and the creature looked over at him. He had a face just like a human; everything was in the same place, only he had two sharp teeth raising from his lower lip and short pointy ears that angled a little more out than they did up.

Seeing Eddie, the creature nodded in his direction and then bolted down the corridor, turning about thirty feet from where it had been standing. The yelling stopped, and Eddie, unable to be shocked any further, shook his head a bit baffled by what he had just seen, and made his way down the hall, where he too came to a stop under the lamp.

"Eddie?" It was the last thing he had expected. At this point, he was confident that nothing else could surprise him today, and yet it happened anyway. Eddie turned to see the woman from the photograph staring at him from behind bars. She was seated at the far corner of the room, holding in her hand the leg of a now broken bed frame. "Eddie, is that you?" the voice said curiously, the woman dropping her makeshift weapon.

How could he not have recognized her in the photograph, it had been nearly ten years, but there was no mistaking that voice. "Camille," Eddie said as he came to grip the bars, staring into the cell at her. There was no mistake. It was his sister.

"Yes, Eddie, it's me," she said, standing from her position in the corner. "I'm going by Emily these days." She walked over to the front of her cage and put her arms through the bars, wrapping them around her brother. "You've grown so much," she said, pulling back away to look him in the face.

She wiped the tears from her eyes and placed her hand on Eddie's cheek as he stood there, staring. "Well, don't just stand there, you lug say something."

Eddie didn't know what to say. The last time he had seen his sister, she was leaving the country to go to grad school. She wrote home maybe twice and then stopped writing altogether.

There was much he wanted to say, some things out of anger and others out of concern. He stayed silent. "I'm sorry, Eddie. I know you must be mad..." She trailed off for a moment and stepped away from him, so they could face each other properly. "I never wanted to hurt you, Eddie, but I had to leave. I was in trouble, and I couldn't risk anything happening to my kid brother."

"Kid brother!" his voice was raised and sudden, and it surprised her. She jumped at the sound of it. "I'm two years older than you. How could you sit there and say you did it to protect me? I spent years looking for you."

Eddie had first met Ray ten years ago, right after Ray founded the Ray Shields Detective Agency and convinced him to help look for his sister who had, in his mind, run off while at college. She was the wilder, more free-spirited of the two of them, and Eddie figured she was off on some adventure experiencing life, but after a year of not hearing from her, he had decided something terrible had happened and enlisted Ray's help.

In the years to follow, he and Ray dedicated a great deal of their time trying to dig up anything they could on her.

"Where did you go?" she asked as if this were news to her.

"I went to Berlin. Where do you think?" Eddie managed to get out.

"I talked to your school and your friends. No one had a clue where you had gone. I started hanging out at nearby bars and clubs and spent my evenings talking to strangers hoping that even one person might have recognized you. Night after night nothing..." It was clear that he was frustrated.

The depth of his voice carried down the halls and in all likely hood to the ears of someone or something that would recognize him as being someone who didn't belong. "Shh, Eddie, you need to be quiet."

* * *

"Quiet!"

I turned, recognizing Eddie's voice through the wall for a second time. He was much louder than when I first heard him, and I realized that I must be getting closer. When I came to the next marked entrance, I pushed the latch, keeping the wall secure and poked my head out.

I was in the middle of a hallway, similar to the ones upstairs, dark and drab. Looking to my right, I saw Eddie standing there, and after peering to the left to make sure we were alone, I stepped out completely. "What do you mean, be quiet?" He raised his voice again, clearly talking to someone.

I pulled the door shut behind me and walked closer. I could see that Eddie was focused on someone on the other side of a cell, and I realized it must be Emily. However, when I heard the trembles in her voice, I knew it was someone who meant much more to him than a damsel in distress. "Eddie, there are people here who are very bad, and you need to keep it down before they find you here."

"She's right, Eddie." He turned to see me standing there. "We're not alone. Every cultist on the grounds is looking for us right now. We need to find a way out of here."

Eddie was upset, to say the least, but he knew I was right. "Fine, but I'm not leaving her locked up. We need to get her out of there," he said, pointing to the cell.

"Already ahead of you." I stepped forward and unlocked the door. "I'll explain later," I said to him, his confused look turning to a more tiresome one as I opened the door. "Right now, we need to be concerned with finding our way out of this dungeon."

Up until now, I hadn't thought about it, but this basement, with all its doors and dark hallways, did kind of feel like a dungeon.

"Any ideas?" I asked, hoping that his time spent down here might have given him a lay of the land, and maybe he would know of a way out.

"Actually, yeah, well maybe." Eddie grabbed his sister by the arm and began to tote her off. It was like he was afraid he would lose her if he wasn't physically holding on to her.

He headed in the direction opposite to which I came, and when he arrived at the corner, he stopped and nodded for me to follow.

"We need to get out of here," he yelled down the hallway, and when I got there and looked, my jaw inadvertently dropped.

"Is that a—" he didn't let me finish my sentence.

"Gargoyle," he said.

"I think so."

He turned back to the creature at the end of the hall and yelled back to it, "Can you show us?"

The creature nodded and turned, looking over its shoulder quickly before going down on all fours and taking off to the right. Eddie tossed a look my way and chirped, "I'll explain later," clearly a jab back at me for my lack of telling him why I had the key.

Together, the three of us made our way through the dark corridors of the compound basement.

Eventually, the hallways began to look less like hallways and more like tunnels. The once smooth concrete walls were now rigid and made natural, and the floor came to be made of dirt rather than stone. I wasn't sure when the shift took place as we were all entirely focused on keeping up with the creature that we hoped was leading us out of here and away from the voices that were now beginning to echo from behind us somewhere.

After what seemed like a very long time running through tunnels, I could see the light beaming from ahead. It was natural light, and I was pretty sure we were headed for the mouth of a cave. The creature stopped a few hundred yards short of the light and waited for us.

As we approached, it bowed, and Eddie thanked it with a nod of his head and a little fist pump. His sister, on the other hand, didn't think too much of the gesture and walked by with her eyes on the little guy as if she didn't trust it. I wasn't sure if I should say anything or just keep walking, and so as I made my way by him, I tried to thank him, but my uncertainty led to a stuttering "thanks, dude," followed by an awkward wave.

As we arrived at the end of the tunnel, the three of us looked back to see the creature, which I was now sure was a gargoyle, disappear into the darkness. "All right, let's not linger about. It's a long drive home, and we still got to figure something out about that tire."

Chapter 6

Finding a ride out from the middle of nowhere proved to be an easier task than she expected. Given that the cultists would soon realize that their guests were no longer on the premises, Eddie and Ray had decided it was best to hide the car somewhere off the road and come back for it at a later time. Camille took to playing lookout while the two wounded men worked to complete the task.

Eventually, the car was hidden; the tracks were covered, and the three of them had made their way back to the main road where, as luck would have it, they were able to wave down an eighteen-wheeler hauling lumber down from the mountain.

The trucker was generous and gave them a lift ten miles out of his way to a small town where Eddie and Ray managed to purchase an old van from one of the locals. He was more than happy to accept the five hundred dollars. A price that was likely more than the car was worth.

The ride was long and quiet. Camille sat in the back seat, staring at her brother. She had positioned herself so that she could see if he would look back at her through the rear-view mirror, but he never did. He just kept on driving, his eyes on the road and nowhere else.

She shifted her attention to Ray. He had managed to dress the gash in his side with a kit from the car and had changed his shirt with an extra that he pulled from a bag in the trunk. She could tell his wounds were bothering him by the way he stirred in his seat, attempting to find a position that didn't cause discomfort. Eventually, she realized she was staring and turned her attention out the window.

There was so much she needed to say, not only to her brother but also to Ray. Things that she had uncovered about her brother's partner, things that were going to change his life and that were connected to the very reason she herself disappeared all those years ago.

"Eddie," she said softly, turning her attention back to the mirror. He didn't respond. Ray looked at him, then back to the road. It was clear that this man understood her brother and, even more clear, that he had a great deal of respect for him.

Ever since they stepped out of the cave, he and Eddie had focused on getting them home without further incident, and as she watched the pair develop a plan, she noted the way in which they listened to each other and the way they worked together as if each were an extension of the other.

She, on the other hand, felt like a third wheel. She had tried to talk to her brother while Ray was changing, but he shrugged her off. It was becoming clear to her that he needed time to take in the events leading up to their reunion. She resolved to sink back into her own thoughts.

She was glad to be free from that horrible place, and she regretted even letting herself get caught. She had been such a fool to get involved with the cult for a second time. She knew it was risky, but she thought enough time had passed, and with the precautions that she had taken, changing her hair color, mastering the Chilean language, and perfecting the accent, not to mention the almost permanent tan she had acquired from all her time in South America, she was so sure that she would be able to infiltrate their ranks and find a way to get her life back.

The woman she had convinced to let her help ruin Bennings had been a junior member in the cult back when she was first introduced to the world of myth and monster, and since she hadn't seen her for who she was, she thought herself safe from being recognized.

Her overconfidence had been a mistake. No sooner had she infiltrated the ranks of the cult than she was discovered in Bennings's office by the magister himself. She was supposed to be in and out, planting fake documents to implement him as selling cult secrets.

Instead, she stuck around trying to dig into a prophecy that she believed could bring about the fall of the cult, a prophecy that a year earlier had led her to discover the whereabouts of the man who would fulfill it, and inadvertently the whereabouts of her brother.

"Camille," Eddie spoke for the first time in nearly two hours. "We're going to be at our office soon. It's late, but we are going to need to talk about how you came to be in that cell."

He looked back at her through the mirror, and she now wished she had been seated out of view. "We can save our conversation for tomorrow."

He sighed and brought his attention back to the road. It was clear he wanted to save what he had to say to her for a more private setting, and possibly for a time when he wasn't as upset. Unfortunately, she knew he wouldn't be getting that opportunity. The two conversations were one and the same. She decided against commenting and instead lay her head back, hoping to collect her thoughts and the courage necessary to have that conversation.

When the car came to a stop, Camille awoke to find that they had reached their destination. Ray stepped out first, opened the van door, and dug back into the front seat, grabbing his charred and bloodstained shirt.

Stepping out, Camille took immediate notice of her surroundings. They were parked in the middle of a gravel drive that circled around what she made for a small airplane hangar. The metal of which was well weathered but structurally looked very sound. A tall chain-link fence enclosed the property and was covered with a black tarp that she initially thought might have been meant to keep prying eyes out.

But when she looked up and around and realized that they were in the middle of the city, surrounded by tall buildings on three sides, she decided that maybe the tarp was meant to keep the eyesore in.

Ray and Eddie walked toward the entrance to the building and opened the door, stepping inside. Neither of them bothered to hold it open for her or even to beckon for her to follow. They were in tune with each other, all right. She stood there for a moment collecting herself, then walked to the door and stepped through it herself.

Inside, she could see the silhouettes of her brother and Ray standing on the other side of a set of milky glass windows that framed the upper half of the wall dividing the room she was standing in from the next. To her immediate left, she found a coat stand with two jackets hanging from it. She recognized Eddie's as he had been wearing it earlier. The other, a longer trench style with a typical gumshoe fedora resting atop, had to be Ray's.

Looking back at the two men, she could see that they were having a somewhat energetic but hushed conversation. "You might want to come back later." Camille turned to see a woman sitting behind a desk to her right. "Somethings got those two in an odd mood." Either they were ignoring all women at the moment, or they simply forgot to tell their secretary that they had a guest.

"Actually, I'm with them."

The woman looked at her for a moment, then stood quickly and made her way around the desk. "Oh, how silly of me. You must be Emily," she said, taking Camille's right hand in both of hers. "I'm Laura."

Before Camille had the chance to correct her, Laura let go of her hand and made her way across the room. "Let me get you some water," she said, taking a glass from the cupboard she was now standing in front of. "Sometimes, I swear these boys forget their manners."

Camille liked this woman already. When Laura returned, she had a glass of water in one hand and a hand towel in the other. "In case you want to clean up a little, there is a washroom just through that door." She pointed in the direction opposite of her. "Go ahead, don't be shy, take your time. I'm sure you must have a lot on your mind right now."

Camille wanted to thank her, but instead, she just smiled and took the offered hand towel. Laura turned and made her way back to her desk.

"Don't worry about them. I'm sure they're going to be a few minutes." She smiled, taking her seat, and picking up a file she had on her desk. Camille watched her briefly, then turned and made her way into the other room without another word.

* * *

I sat at my desk watching Eddie pace the length of my office, and I couldn't help but notice that he hadn't bothered pouring himself a drink. I understood his preoccupations were weighing heavily on him, but I would have thought the matters at hand would have driven him straight to the bottle. My partner was a good man, and while he did have a good deal of control, he, like any other alcoholic, was known to turn to the remedy of pouring himself a bath of whiskey for the soaking pleasure of his thoughts.

"I just don't get it, Ray. We spent years looking for her, chasing even the smallest clues halfway around the world, and nothing. Ten years it's been Ray, ten years. How does one just walk away from everything, from everyone? And to never look back, that's just bullshit."

He stopped pacing just long enough to look over at the mini-bar, then promptly went back to wearing the varnish off the floor between the couch and my desk.

In all the years we've known each other, I'd only ever seen him this agitated once. It was just after we arrived back from chasing another fruitless lead on the case of his missing sister. No sooner had we stepped out of the airport than some poor bloke made the mistake of commenting on Eddie's clearly visible lack of cheer.

Long story short, the man's luggage wound up under the wheels of a passing airport taxi, and he, who was only moments earlier cheerful as a kid reveling in the freedom of being ungrounded, was quickly taken into custody when the contents of his exploded bag revealed that he had just smuggled in an entire Kilo of cocaine. I guess the dogs were off duty that day.

Luckily, the police took our status as private investigators as our catching someone they missed and sent us on our way with no questioning.

The recollection of Eddie's past tantrum kept me silent through the tirade, and though I feared for the safety of my office furniture, well most of it, I couldn't afford to let him stew any longer in the company of his own thoughts. "You can be as mad as you want, Eddie!" I said as he came to stand closest to the chair that I, or anyone else for that matter, had yet to figure out how to properly use. "But she's tied up in this all the same."

He placed his hands on the edge of the chair's backrest, and for a moment, as I watched his large fingers dig into the orange fabric, I thought this was finally the end of the rather uncomfortable but somehow stylish piece of seating. Eddie released his grip and walked over to the chair next to my desk, taking a seat.

I frowned at the missed opportunity to rid myself of the chair and looked back at him. "I know this isn't the ideal reunion, Eddie, but at least she's back." He sat there silently, staring out the window over my shoulder. "Are you hearing me, Eddie? You have your sister ba…"

Before I could even finish the statement, Eddie's voice boomed over mine. "You think I don't know that, Ray!" He retorted. "That's just it, damn it. We spent all those years looking for her, and then one day, that day we got back from Peru, it all came clear to me. She was gone, Ray, and I was never going to see her again. Get it? I gave up on her."

Eddie buried his face in his hands for a moment, then brushed them off to the side. I could see that it was going to take him much longer to heal from the shock of his sister's return than it would for either of us to recover from our wounds following the encounter with the Cynanthrope, Valora.

He took in a deep breath, rose, and then glanced over at my office bar. Certain that this would be the moment that he reached for a drink. I began to rise from my seat to join him, but he instead walked over to the cart and poured himself a tall glass of water. I debated whether or not to comment on the curiosity, but the decision was made for me when the door to my office opened, and Laura's head popped in.

From her current angle, I was the only one visible to her, but that didn't stop Eddie from straightening up and bringing his face into its usual composure. He may have been willing to let his guard down with me, but he certainly was not about to do so in front of Laura. "I know you two are busy right now, but you've kept the poor miss Emily out here waiting for nearly twenty minutes."

"Right," I replied, looking over to Eddie. He shared the same look of realization with me that we had never told Laura who our guest really was. He nodded, and I looked back to Laura. "OK," I said. "Why don't you bring her in here, and the both of you have a seat?"

"Right indeed," she said, ducking out briefly, returning with Camille in tow.

The pair made their way to the couch, and once Laura finished clearing a spot on the sofa, they took a seat. Eddie maintained his standing position near the drink cart, and I seated myself beside Laura in the matching leather chair that sat at the far end of the table.

"Laura—" I paused to collect my thoughts. "I guess I need to make a proper introduction, now don't I?" I said.

"Don't be silly Ray, Emily and I got ourselves acquainted while the two of you were back here being all secretive and whatnot."

"Damn it, her name isn't Emily."

Eddie's voice, though not raised, still roared in the stillness of the room. "It's Camille. Her name is Camille, and she's my sister."

"Sister," Laura said, looking over to Camille, then to Eddie, then back over to Camille. "Oh!" she said, sitting back but keeping her straight posture. "I can see it now. In fact, now that I see it, I can't believe I missed it."

Laura had a point. Being aware of the relation did make it hard not to see the resemblance. Eddie's clean-shaved face and tidy combover radiated with confidence, and though his square jawline and deeply set eyes served in most cases to intimidate those who might set out to size him up, at this moment, they only served to give him away.

Camille was beautiful. The shade of her long brown hair, at least at the roots, matched Eddie's, and her face, while definitely more attractive, projected a presence of strength and determination. It was clear that the jawline and deeply laid eyes ran in the family, and it was possible that if one were to go back and thumb through historic family photos, that every ancestor would share the same stoic facial traits.

"I'm sorry," Camille said, looking at Laura. "There just wasn't a moment to tell you." Laura simply smiled at her, acknowledging that the apology was unnecessary.

Seeing an opportunity to move past the awkwardness of the situation, I cleared my throat, gathering the attention of my colleagues and our guest.

"Camille," I said, directing my attention to her. "We need to know how you got yourself mixed up with this cult. We have some understanding as to what you were doing there, well, at least what you were supposed to be doing for Ms. Valentine, but beyond that, we have nothing, so anything you can share would really help us."

Looking at Eddie, she sighed. "I'm sorry, Eddie. I never meant to hurt you," she paused, and as I looked over at him, I could see he was maintaining his dour face.

"The cult, Camille," I said.

"I know," she replied. "I was getting there." She leaned forward, rested her forearms atop her knees, and began to rub her hands together. "Ten years ago, shortly after I arrived in Europe, I befriended a girl named Jillian Stone. She was also attending school far from home, and the two of us hit it off instantly. We rented an apartment together, worked at the same pizza parlor, and once we even wound up dating the same guy."

Eddie looked at her disapprovingly. "Separately, of course," she said in response to his action. "Jillian was amazing. She was a free spirit, and there was never a moment with her that was dull," she sighed, glanced around the room, and then continued.

"For a while, everything was going just like I had imagined it would. School was great. I had a job I liked, friends, a great roommate. Then, as fast as it all began, it ended."

Camille stopped the repetitive motion of her hands and sat back, her straight posture now matching Laura's. "Jillian came home one night looking rattled, and when I tried to get her to tell me what was wrong, she just shrugged me off."

"After that night, things were never the same. She grew distant, our outings became less frequent, and though I wanted to ask her about that night many times over, I just couldn't bring myself to do so. I guess I thought that whatever it was, she would either tell me when she was ready, or she would eventually move past it, and things would go back to normal."

"Oh, you poor dear," Laura interrupted, placing her hand on Camille's shoulder.

Camille looked at her, smiled at the gesture, then put her head back down and continued, "Eventually, things did begin to feel normal again, and one day Jillian invited me to hang out with some friends that she had made. I assumed that she was trying to rekindle what we had lost and that this was her way of apologizing, so naturally, I accepted her offer."

Camille stopped talking, took a breath, stood up, walked around the table, and came to stand in front of us.

"That was the first time I met Allister Bennings."

Upon hearing mention of the cult leader's name, all three of us sitting before Camille stirred in our chairs and made ready to give our full attention to her.

"Back then, he was going by Alli, and he was, according to Jillian, the most handsome and charming man that she had ever met. That evening when she introduced us, I thought maybe she was just a notch on his belt, but she really liked him, and we weren't as close as we used to be, so I felt that it wasn't my place to say anything.

"Jillian and I had met up with Alli and a few of his friends at the train station, where we caught a train out to the country. She told me that we would be spending the weekend at Allister's father's ranch and that I would really like it there.

"It wasn't until after the two-hour train ride and forty minutes of riding in a van that I realized that she herself had never been. When we arrived at this so-called ranch, I was surprised to see that it was more of a compound than a ranch and that the mood that everyone was once in had shifted to a more serious one.

"I tried telling Jillian that something wasn't right, but she wouldn't listen. When we entered the largest of the three buildings, I tried to run but was grabbed by Allister, and he assured me that everything was going to be all right.

"I didn't know what to make of what I saw, let alone think of a way to escape his grasp, so I just kept walking. He ushered me around with his hand on my arm while he spoke about all the mysterious beasts that surrounded us. Stall after stall, cage after cage, we walked down corridors filled with creatures I had never seen before.

"It was all so disorienting and confusing that I didn't realize that the number of people with us had increased, that is, until we arrived in a large room with a staircase that spiraled up to some kind of stone pulpit. At that point, I realized there were some thirty people gathered at its base, most of whom were wearing gray robes with dark green trim and a gold M shape on the chest."

As I sat listening to Camille recap the details of her past, I couldn't help noticing the anger on Eddie's face. I knew it wasn't visible to anyone other than myself, but it was there, somewhere behind the seriousness that he wore to keep it hidden from view. He looked at me briefly, and I, for one reason or another, turned my attention back to Camille.

"I tried fighting Allister's grip, but he held firm, and my actions only caused another man to grab hold of my other arm. I would have fought back more had it not been for Jillian. She kept saying I was overreacting and that I should listen to what they had to say. Then she put on her own gray robe and turned to face the pulpit with the others.

"I knew at that moment that I had lost her and that if I was going to get out of there, it was going to be alone. A few minutes later, a man shows up and climbs the stairs to the pulpit. He gives a little speech about the importance of being charges of the dark and some spiel about the need for growth.

"After he finished, he made his way down from the pulpit and over to Jillian and me. It didn't take him but a second to see that she was already on board with his twisted message, so he paid her little attention beyond letting her kiss his hand and turned his focus onto me. That's when everything got ugly."

"Ugly," I said curiously.

"Yeah, ugly," she said with a sigh, staring back at me. "He said disbelievers had to be made to understand the power that the darkness held over the light, and then he proceeded to walk through his herd before stopping in front of a young red-headed boy of about sixteen. He handed him a key and spoke in French for a moment, then gave him a nod."

Laura's eyebrow furrowed in response to hearing this little bit, and I made a mental note to ask her about it later. "The next thing I know, the kid was unlocking a gate to the nearest enclosure in the room. He stepped inside and secured the door before making his way to the center of it."

She paused. It was a long pause, and while such a silent moment might in any other situation have been awkward, this silence only served to intensify our current state of curiosity.

"He stood there," she said. "He held his arms out in front of him, extended them at his side, and turned to face us. That's when I saw it. What I thought to be a giant rock sitting in the center of the enclosure stood and revealed itself to be a monster. It was a solid thirty feet of hulking mass. The poor kid didn't stand a chance. The rock-like monster made a deep bellowing sound and swung down, smashing the kid into the ground."

Camille bowed her head. "Everyone in the room was covered in a shower of blood, and with that, I fainted. The last thing I saw was Jillian's face as her eyes widened. She looked so—enthralled by it all. When I awoke, I was back on the train with her and Allister."

"Wait, they let you go?" Laura's inquiry was shared by all of us, though Eddie's interest was most apparent.

"No, I wasn't going anywhere. Allister made it clear to me that if I tried to run or told anyone about that night, he would kill Jillian and come after me. I know Jilli and I weren't exactly friends anymore, but I couldn't bring myself to be responsible for such a thing."

Eddie snapped at her. "So, you carried on like you had no one to turn to!" His voice was deep, but I could tell he was keeping it all under control.

"No, I carried on knowing that I had to be cautious, or everyone I ever cared for would become a victim of these people." Her response was equally fierce and composed. Eddie's expression, while still neutral to the girls, told me that he was beyond furious right now.

Though I was almost sure it was not with Camille, his anger likely rested with Mr. Bennings. Camille looked at her brother as if she only now truly understood how badly she had wounded him. "I did what I felt I had to do," she said, looking back at Laura and me, continuing her story.

"Over the next two years, I began to let on that I was coming around to the ways of the cult, and while it was all a mask on my part, things between Jillian and I got better. I had to make sure Allister and the others didn't see me as a threat if I was going to stand a chance at getting out of there and protecting those I cared about.

"I attended gatherings all over Europe, being careful to never ask too many questions, and I learned as much as they wanted me to about the beasts in cages and those that walked among us."

Camille's comment about those that walk among us stirred the memory of Valora. In human form, one would have never thought of her as having the ability to transform into a ten-foot-tall beast. In fact, the only thing a person might have to say about her was that she needed a fashion makeover.

"Eventually, they let their guard down, and I was accepted. I even had Allister fooled to the point that he started to turn his attention more to me and away from Jilli. Hmmm," she scoffed at the thought.

"One evening, Allister came to me and asked that I meet with him and a few of the others. The first thing I noticed when I arrived was that Jilli wasn't there. When I asked him about it, he told me that the conversation we were going to have had to remain secret and that he didn't want to take the risk of her letting slip any part of it," she sighed.

"I didn't think much of the comment at first. I thought he was just trying to get closer to me. He sure proved me wrong."

Camille walked over to my office window, peeling apart the shades to look out onto the orange glow of the lamp that lit the gravel drive encircling the office.

"Allister claimed that he alone held power to bring the cult to its full potential and that the current magister was a fool and knew nothing of the true power of the darkness. Not everyone he had invited was one of his underlings, so this comment immediately divided the room. In fact, the majority of those present were very loyal to Magister Henson and were ready to leave right then and there. Allister's next action quickly put a stop to that."

Camille removed her finger from the shades and turned back to face us. "He stood before the cultists and pulled from his robe a medallion with the symbol of Monstre on it. The crowd of disgruntled cultists promptly took their seats and listened to what he had to say."

"Before you continue," I said, interrupting her at the pinnacle of her story, my action clearly displeasing Laura, who was now glaring at me for the intrusion. I ignored the scowl and walked over to my desk, retrieving the photographs I had received in the mail. "Is this the medallion that you're talking about?" I asked, handing her the picture of the strange coin.

"Yes, this is it," she said, a bit confused by my having the photograph. "This medallion dates to the rise of the cult and is said to have been a gift to the first magister by the Dark Lord himself and to contain the power of its creator. That's how the cult got its name Monstre de Ténèbres, it's French for—"

"Monster of darkness," Laura said, finishing Camille's sentence.

Camille looked at Laura for a moment, recognizing the fluency in her pronunciation. Though Laura's accent was not as strong as it had once been, whenever she did speak her mother tongue it became very obvious that she was a French woman through and through.

Camille nodded, acknowledging Laura's accurate translation, then continued. "Of course, the medallion was believed to have been lost a very long time ago when the fourth magister Tamile fled persecution from an angry town that had suffered the wrath of a large bear-like beast, a beast he was seen observing only a few days before. Apparently, the monster had come into town during a harvest celebration and carried away ten children in its teeth."

Eddie and I glanced at each other briefly as we recalled the massive bear head that hung on the wall in the mansion and the rug on which we had set our feet. "The magister claimed to have used the medallion to kill the uncontrollable beast, but in doing so, the medallion was torn from his neck. And despite all the searching, it was never found, that is until Allister came into possession of it."

"Wait a minute," Eddie said, interrupting her. "Let me get this straight, the medallion was lost centuries ago, and somehow this Bennings's character stumbles across it. Surely no one bought that."

"For about thirty seconds, yes, there was doubt," she responded. "A few of the cultists voiced their concern, but he just smiled at them, put the medallion around his neck and pulled out a small book from his robe, and began to read from it. He then lifted the medallion and faced the loudest of those who opposed him. The man was disintegrated right there in front of all of us. All that remained was the ash in his seat and the particles that floated through the air. I can assure you, Eddie, the medallion is the real deal."

Convinced by the sternness of his sister's voice, he retreated to his silent self and let her continue. "Allister claimed to have come across a letter written by the fourth magister tucked away in the archives and after following some instruction came to find the medallion and the book which he held, buried beneath a lone grave in the middle of the Landes Forest in France.

"He was convinced that the Dark Lord wanted him to find the medallion, that he had been chosen to lead the cult on an undertaking that would bring about the apocalypse, and that it would take place somewhere in South America."

"After that, things became chaotic. Allister gathered the support of the majority and staged a coup. I knew that I wouldn't get another chance to get away, so, days leading up to the takeover, I made arrangements to fake my death and leave the country," Camille sighed and returned to sit around the table.

"It was easier than you would imagine," she said. "When Allister made his move, I let loose a few of the beasts, and once they had killed a few of the members, I found the body of a young female who was about my height, that, due to the nature of her death was unrecognizable, and put my necklace on her. I then left during the disorder and caught a train into Spain, then a flight to South America."

"South America," Eddie said, staring at her in disbelief. "It sounds to me like you could have come home."

"I wanted to," she replied. "But knowing Allister, they would have come looking for me just to be certain I was dead."

Camille let out a sigh and continued, "I knew I couldn't go home, so I did the only thing I could think to do; get ahead of Allister and find out what he was planning. I landed in Peru and took a bus through Bolivia and into Chile. To be honest, I really wasn't sure where I should start my investigation, so I just found the first library I could and started reading up on the local myths and religions."

"A sound place to start, I think."

Camille smiled at my attempt to lighten the mood. Eddie wasn't as pleased with the comment. "It was six months before I found my first real clue. According to the

Mapuche people, they're an indigenous tribe of Indians native to Chile," she explained.

"There once existed an evil so great that the tribe was forced to sacrifice their daughters in order to keep from being destroyed. The being was known as the Cherufe, a monster made of magma and stone that resided in a volcano. Their god Antu, seeing the daughters of his people being killed in such a manner, sent two of his warrior daughters to imprison the Cherufe by arming them with magical swords made of ice."

Camille paused to take a breath, and I looked over to my partner to see how he was taking all of this. While it was clear that Eddie still harbored an ill attitude, the mention of magical swords must have amused him because the look on his face was a cross between disbelief and 'hell I've seen so much today that shouldn't be possible, so why not.'

Either way, the relaxed look on his face was welcome. "I know it sounds like a fairy tale," she continued, "and that's what I thought too, but since I didn't have much to go on and since everything I had been through lately had taught me to expect the unexpected, I set out to try and confirm the legend.

"I spent the better part of a year between Chile and Argentina searching for a man named Cairo, a visual Anthropologist whose work about Gran Terremoto de Chile centered around the hardship brought to the Mapuche tribes following the quake. Cairo not only presented a first-hand account of the disaster.

"He also claims that the Machi of the tribe that housed him took him on a spiritual journey where he was confronted with a grave truth that he had no choice but to publish. This publication cost him his credibility and thereafter, his job. He disappeared shortly after being discredited, but the local belief was that he was somewhere in the Andes Mountains searching for proof of his claim.

"Things were difficult that first year. My evenings were spent learning to speak Spanish, and my days were spent butchering the language. Eventually, I got to a stage where I could make sense of the stories I was being told and discovered that Cairo had first traveled south to a volcano known as Fueguino or Vulcan Cook. I spent a few months looking for him, traveling from one volcano to the next until I finally caught up with him."

Camille's accounts were unsettling, and as unbelievable as this all seemed, the fatigue that showed on her face was enough to convince me that whatever had transpired since her disappearance all those years ago, she was telling the truth about dedicating her life to a seemingly impossible venture.

"He was living like a hermit between two villages," she continued. "and he wanted nothing to do with me until I explained why I was there. After that, the man seemed to have a revived sense of purpose, and the next thing I know, I'm being handed handwritten manuscripts, pictures, and maps with all kinds of scribblings and Xs covering them.

"It was his life's work and moving forward, it pretty much became mine. Finding and convincing him to help me boosted my belief that I might be able to stop Allister, but the next few years would take that confidence away from me."

Camille rubbed her eyes with her hands, then placed them on the back of the same chair Eddie's had rested on earlier.

"All of our efforts to discover the location of the Cherufe's prison were met with obstacle after obstacle. Every time we found something that might lead us there, it would turn out to be hearsay or altogether a lie. Once, we even spent two days descending into a volcano looking for a cave that was said to house the remains of the sword that struck the final blow."

Camille blew the hair from her face. "That also proved fruitless, and eventually, we both decided to put an end to our search, and we were on our way down from the mountain when we were caught in a rockslide. Cairo was buried under a mountain of debris, and I was left injured and alone.

"For two days, I was alone on what was left of that mountain path, waiting to die. In fact, I even reached a point where I thought I did. That's when I was found by a man who had come to survey the damage and was taken back to his village healer." She paused again and took another breath. "And that's how I wound up here."

"I think you're leaving something out," I said, pointing out her previous housing situation.

"I am, and I'm not," she said. "Let me be more clear. A ceremony called Machitun was performed by the Machi to help heal me. In the process, she and I were given a shared vision. It was honestly the most terrible thing I have ever experienced."

Camille sat down at the far end of the table. "The world as we know it was ash," she said, her voice now beginning to show signs of distress. "Everything was on fire, and smoldering city after city, the world was void of life. In the vision, the Machi was standing at my side. Her eyes were as black as the smoke that rose around us, and when she spoke, I was overcome with fear."

Camille looked at the three of us with a great deal of intensity before she said her final bit. "She said that a great evil would soon beset the earth. That he would rise from fire and brimstone, and that no one would be spared his fury."

Camille's eyes welled with tears, but her voice didn't waver. The Machi's next words were her last. 'But fear not, child,' she said, 'there is a chance. For a shield will stand against the darkness, sword in hand. And he will succeed or fail; his fate is hers.'

Camille took to remaining silent again and then directed her attention toward me. "She prophesied that this end could be stopped by only one person. 'A shield standing against the darkness, sword in hand'." She grits her teeth, the tears now flowing freely from her face. "She was talking about you, Ray. You are the shield. You are the only chance we have to prevent the end of all life as we know it."

Chapter 7

The information Camille shared about the cult had been enough to convince Ray that a trip was in order, and Laura had been in the process of redeeming the air mileage the boys had racked up over the years, when Ray stopped her, insisting that they keep a lower profile and fly by way of a cargo plane.

"So much for keeping a low profile," she said to herself, now sitting some twenty-eight thousand feet in the sky aboard a Lockheed Martin C130 piloted by non-other than the great Hurston Pierce himself.

Hurston and Ray went back a ways, and Ray, on more than one occasion, made mention of a debt that could never be repaid. Laura still had no idea how Hurston came to owe Ray on such a scale, but it wasn't his connection to Ray that worried her. What worried her was his means of coming to own this customized behemoth of a plane and the numerous estates that were under the Pierce name. Well, the status that came with his success, anyway.

Hurston had acquired a fortune, small in no measure, after inadvertently discovering a treasure trove of artifacts and lost art while scaling a mountain near Neuschwanstein castle. He had been attempting to find a good vantage from which to descend in his flight suit when he came across the cave.

Long story short, he made headlines after a picture of him was taken with a missing Van Gogh tied to his chest as he soared across the Bavarian sky. That Photo, and the press that came after, made Hurston Pierce a global celebrity. She was worried that if the cult were so well connected, they would most definitely be aware of Ray's connections and find a way to use it against him.

Ray was currently in the cockpit with Hurston and had been for most of the trip, while Camille and Eddie were busy catching up at the far end of the cargo hold. This left Laura to sink into her own thoughts. She wondered what validity there was to Camille's vision. The poor girl had been near death, after all.

Then, recalling her own vivid dreams, she dismissed her disbelief. Instead, she turned her thoughts to the prophecy. If what Camille said was true, then this evil she spoke of was the beast that Allister was trying to resurrect, and if Ray were the shield that would, as Camille put it, stand against the darkness, then who the hell was her that held Ray's fate in their hands.

Whoever she was, Laura didn't like the idea of Ray's well-being being in the hands of anyone other than Eddie's. She sighed at the thought of it all and got up to stretch her legs. "One benefit of not flying coach," she said to herself as she made her way to one of the starboard side portholes.

Outside, the day faded, and the clouds that blanketed the sky beneath them had grown dark. The horizon, red from the setting sun, resembled that of a flame, and Laura, in her effort to clear her head, couldn't help but imagine the world as Camille had described it in her vision.

She tried shifting her focus off both the clouds and the horizon, but she was unable to look away, and the fiery scene below began to transform into something more. The clouds burst to life, rolling, and swirling in the most unnatural of ways, and Laura, who only moments before stood safely aboard the Hurston Hercules, felt herself pulled from her own being.

She looked around only to see that neither the plane nor the sky was there, and below her, the earth smoldered as far as the eye could see.

"Laurrrra," She froze, shuddering at the sound of the raspy voice. "Come to me, Laurrrra." She tried bringing her eyes off the blackened land below but couldn't. "You will be mine, Laurrrra." The voice came from all around her. Desperate to not hear it again, she raised her head to face whatever it was.

"Laura—Laura, is everything OK?" Camille was standing beside her now, her hand on Laura's shoulder. "You were gone there for a minute."

Laura looked back out the window briefly. The sun had set, and the sky outside was pitch black. "Yes, I'm fine," she said, looking at Camille with a smile. "Eddie went to see how much longer till we get there. I must say he's grown to be quite the man."

Laura couldn't imagine how Camille must have felt finally getting to see her brother after all this time, but years of watching Eddie drink to hide his own pain gave her a pretty good idea of the kind of struggle she went through. "Yes, he's quite the gentleman when he wants to be,"

Camille returned the compliment of her brother with a smile.

"We're still a few hours out, ladies," Hurston said as he clamored down the ladder leading to the cockpit. "Best you get some rest before we get there. Who knows what kind of strange things are going to be there waiting for you." Camille and Laura shared a brief look of concern before Hurston assured them the plane was in good hands. "The planes on autopilot; besides, Eddie is not a bad choice for copilot."

"Copilot?" Camille said. "You mean Eddie knows how to fly a plane too." She looked back at Laura.

"Don't look at me. I had no idea he could fly a plane."

"Knows how to fly a plane. That's an understatement, sweetheart. When you get a chance, ask him about Peru."

Laura didn't much care for being called sweetheart, but she could tell Hurston's comment was harmless, and she decided to let him off the hook, with express instructions not to let it slip again. "Mr. Pierce, if you would be so kind as to refrain from calling me sweetheart for the remainder of the flight, I'd greatly appreciate it."

"Sure thing sw—I mean, of course."

Hurston bowed his head and walked over to a wall just forward of the rear door. "It's not much," he said, reaching up to release two latches above the metal bulkhead. "But it's better than sleeping in the chairs." Hurston took a step back, and the bulkhead lowered to reveal a pair of Murphy bunk beds hidden behind it. "There are only two of these babies, so I suggest you ladies take 'em."

Laura was exhausted, and the beds certainly looked inviting, though the shell that had hidden them was metal, and the mattress didn't look too comfortable. "Maybe later," she said. "For now, Hurston, why don't you tell Camille here all about your climb to glory, or shall we say your dive?"

Hurston gave a wide, if not crooked smile and replied. "Most certainly, it's always been one of my favorites."

* * *

"Say, Ray, what do you think about all this?" Eddie had come up to the cockpit under the guise of giving Hurston a chance to stretch his legs, but I knew he had a different motive.

"I think you should trust her, Eddie," I said, turning my attention from the darkness outside to him. He flipped a switch on the dashboard and grunted. "We've seen far too much in the past few days to suggest that any part of her story is a lie. Besides, I think we have bigger things to worry about."

"You mean like you being the only thing that stands between Allister and the end of the world."

"Yeah," I replied. "Like that." Eddie was clearly amused, but the thought of a prophecy foretelling the potential total destruction of the world with only me to prevent it was a bit disconcerting. A week ago, I would have laughed at the idea. Now all I could do was try to keep my mind off of it.

I remained silent past his ragging remark, but the stillness of the space didn't match that of my mind. "We're really out of our league here, Eddie," I said finally. "Even with your sister's knowledge on our side, we don't have much in the way of preventing the end of the world."

"Sure we have, Ray. We have you."

"I'm not kidding around here, Eddie." He paused at the sternness in my voice.

"I know, Ray, but at least we know that Allister needs the amulet to raise this thing, and we know he's going to be in Chile. So, we just have to stop him from using it."

"Easier said than done," I replied. "We still need to find the right volcano."

"Actually, I was thinking about that, and I had an idea. The last time we were in Peru, one of the maps in that bar we were at was for the rail system in Chile. If I remember correctly, the rail line is quite extensive and runs not only the length of the country but passes through the Andes and goes right by several volcanoes. I'd say we have a pretty good chance of finding out where he's going if we follow that railroad."

I could see Eddie was running the list of bars we visited in Peru through his head rather than thinking about the maps themselves. "You know, Eddie, when we get there, getting those maps is going to be one of the first things we need to do," I said.

"Yea, so." His response was a little shocking. I'd never known Eddie to turn down an opportunity to get a drink, and now it's happened twice in two days. "Nothing, just that we need to get 'em is all."

"You boys all right up here?" Hurston had made his way back into the cockpit, relieving Eddie of his seat and me of the awkward moment with my partner.

"Fine," Eddie said as he got up from Hurston's chair and made his way out of the cabin. "What was that all about?"

"Beats me," I said, turning my attention back to the controls. My feigned ignorance, clearly unbelievable.

* * *

Laura looked up from her conversation with Camille as Eddie made his way over to them. She was about to ask him how Ray was when the plane shook violently. Hurston's head poked through the cabin door as he hollered back at the trio. "You three better find something to hold on to; looks like the rest of this trip is going to get a little rough."

Eddie made an attempt at reaching the nearest porthole when the plane shook again. This time violent enough to cause all three of them to lose their footing and send them tumbling toward the rear of the plane. Laura was closest to the window, and as she and the others attempted to gain their footing, she nearly lost hers out of sheer shock.

Outside, the cloudless sky was dark, void of stars or anything that one could expect to see while flying at nearly thirty thousand feet. For a moment, she wondered if they were even in the air or trapped in some void of nothingness. A flash of lightning and a shadowy figure revealed that they were far from alone.

"Oh—My—God."

Laura backed away from the window while the others leaned in for a look. Cursing could be heard coming from the cockpit, followed by an almost panicked Hurston yelling, "Hold on!"

Suddenly the plane pitched to the right. Eddie had managed to grab ahold of Camille and the cargo netting next to him just in time to prevent the both of them from being thrust across the plane. Laura was not so fortunate.

She had only just managed to begin to comprehend what she had just seen when Hurston yelled, and she hadn't anytime to make it close enough to anything that she could hang on to. The force of the impact against the port-side wall was excruciating, but there wasn't time to feel the pain. Every window in the hold lit up, and the sky outside ignited. And as the plane once again began to maneuver quickly, she grabbed hold of the Cargo net and held on for her life.

The walls of the plane began to spin, and she suddenly felt this weightless sensation as the plane started to dive and rotate. Laura could see that Eddie and Camille were doing the same, each holding on for their lives as the plane pitched and yawed and rolled.

The walls of the plane seemed to get hotter and hotter with each passing of light outside, and she knew why. She wondered if the others did as well. A brief moment of level flying and shared glances told her that they did. The shadowy figure that she had seen, the fire-like lighting outside the windows, the heating of the plane; they were sharing the sky with a dragon.

Just then, Hurston came barreling out of the cockpit, making his way to the very back of the plane. "You three get strapped in now," he said in an almost too calm voice.

"Strapped in?" Eddie questioned. "Wouldn't we be better off putting on some parachutes and getting out of this matchbox?"

The look on Hurston's face hinted at his displeasure of hearing his plane being compared to a matchbox, but the comment and smirk that followed clearly pleased him to deliver. "There aren't enough parachutes, Eddie." Eddie scowled at him. "In fact, there is only one. And it belongs to my flight suit. So, unless you want to be the one to play decoy, I suggest you get strapped in."

"Decoy," Eddie said, with a puzzled look on his face. "What do you mean decoy?"

Hurston had wasted no time in pulling his flight suit from a bag stashed behind yet another bulkhead. "I mean, that thing out there isn't going to stop until it brings us out of the sky."

It was clear in how quickly he had the suit dawned and his helmet strapped that Hurston was no newbie to the art of flying without a plane, but to face off against a dragon was suicide. "You don't think you're seriously going to stand a chance out there, do you?"

"Like I said, he ain't gonna stop." Hurston made his way to the rear of the hold and pressed the button to the intercom. "Now, Ray," he said before advising the others to hold tight.

The door at the tail of the plane lifted, and once it was fully open, pressed against the fire-lit sky, was the silhouette of Hurston in his flight suit. "The com came on, and Ray could be heard."

"Safe Flying H," he said.

"You just land my plane in one piece," Hurston yelled back.

Without another word, Hurston extended his arms and dropped down through the opening. Eddie Camille and

Laura all leaned over to see him zip through the air and bear down on the burning sky behind them. Then without warning, the massive head of their pursuer burst through the clouds ahead of Hurston, and just as quickly, the rest of the beast came to be.

"Ho—ly—Hell—" Eddie fumbled to get the words out of his mouth. The dragon was much larger than the Hercules, and it was only now that Eddie and the others realized that Hurston had been right.

As they watched, the dragon reared back, using its wings to break mid-flight. The abrupt stop and forward flapping of his wings rocked the plane, yet Hurston seemed to be unaffected by the gusts.

Like an aerobatic knight, he charged head-on towards the monster. Fearless and forward, his aim seemingly to be straight into the belly of the beast. Camille gasped as the dragon pulled its head back in what could only be seen as the readying of a strike. Then, just as the dragon thrust its head forward, releasing a stream of fire that soared hundreds of feet across the sky, Hurston banked left and came to travel parallel to the blazing trail, his path seemingly unaltered.

"He's crazy," Camille said. The shocked expression on her face was evident, through the tremble in her voice.

"Eddie, I could use you up here," Ray's Voice boomed over the intercom.

"Right," Eddie responded. "All right, guys, do what he said and get strapped in. We're going to be making an emergency descent. We need to get out of the air and use every second he's giving us."

The three of them took one last look out the now-closing tail door to see what looked like Hurston pulling something from his side and throwing it at the dragon just as he swept past the beast's head. The plane began to bank and slowly lose altitude.

"Eddie," Ray yelled again, and with that, Eddie Hastily made his way back to the cockpit to help his partner fly the plane.

Chapter 8

Hurston was an excellent pilot, and arguably, he was even better flying in his suit. Whether or not he was good enough to battle a dragon, I couldn't say, but as Eddie and I had begun making our descent, the sky behind us rocked one explosion after another.

Eventually, the thunderous sound and bright flashes faded, and then the sky went still. I wasn't sure what fate my friend had been granted, and at the moment, I didn't have the time to really think about it. What I did know was that Hurston had at the very least managed to land a few punches while in aerial combat with a dragon, a feat in itself, and he succeeded in permitting the rest of us to get out of there safely.

While I hadn't been on board with Hurston going out to face off with a master of the sky, he and I both knew that the only way the plane was landing on our terms was if something could be done to buy us time. Hurston bought us that time by using his flight suit and a few remote-detonated C4 charges. Where he obtained the C4, I didn't know, but he had it nonetheless.

Eddie and I had managed to land the plane without further incident thanks to Hurston, and I could only hope that the dragon wasn't the victor of their dogfight.

While Eddie and Camille were working on securing some maps of the rail system and finding us a way of getting out of the city as discreetly as possible, I was currently tending Laura's wounds in a small room of your typical slum-like motel.

"How does that feel?" I asked, removing the ice from her side and applying a little pressure to her ribs. "Well, it certainly doesn't feel very good." She scoffed. "I know it's unpleasant, but your breathing doesn't seem to be hindered, and it doesn't feel like you've broken any ribs, so I'm gonna go out on a limb here and say you're just going to have one nasty bruise."

Laura clearly didn't like the idea of being sore for the next few weeks, but she was tougher than she looked, and I knew without a doubt that she wouldn't let the injury impede the group's efforts. And it was for this reason, it was going to be my responsibility to make sure she got enough rest.

"Just relax for now," I said, stuffing an extra pillow behind her so that she could be seated upright. "Camille and Eddie are going to be a while; besides, you and I have a few things to talk about."

She raised her eyebrow at me, and I responded by tilting my head before commenting. "You haven't exactly been yourself lately, and I know nothing has been normal, but the day this all began, you weren't at work. You've never been late before, let alone missed an entire day, and don't think I haven't taken notice of your looks of curiosity toward some of what Camille said."

Laura sat up on the bed and grimaced a little at the pain. For a moment, I could see she was considering her words or, rather, if she was going to say anything at all. After a few moments, she went ahead and let it out. "It's back, Ray," she said.

I didn't have to ask to know what she was talking about. The look in her eyes when she said it brought me right back to the first day we met, and I could see the same look of distress in her now as I did back then. "I'm sorry, Laura, I should have realized," I said, sitting up from my somewhat slouched position on the bed. "When we get back, provided the world doesn't end first, Eddie and I will make sure the guy is gone for good this time."

"No, Ray," she said. "You don't understand. It's not a person." The confusion on my face was clear, and she responded in like. "I don't understand it either, but I'm certain now that whatever is going on with the cult and Camille and this prophecy, it's all connected to what's happening to me."

My confusion by her announcement only grew, but I trusted Laura, and I had a strange feeling that whatever was going on, the truth would be revealing itself sometime in our near future. So, I sat listening to her recollections of the visions and her description of the voice that haunted her.

"So, what do you make of the inscription?" I asked.

"Honestly, I'm not sure what to make of it," she said. "Maybe it's just symbolic of the cult's knowledge of the truth and their desire to literally raise Hell. But I think I'm more worried about this Cherufe and why I am being called to it."

Given the intensity of her visions, the frequency that she was hearing this voice, and our newfound understanding of what's real in this world, she definitely had reason to fear her connection.

"Look, Laura, I know we don't have a lot of answers right now, but now that you've shared this with me, maybe we can talk to Camille about it an—"

"No!" she said abruptly. "Please, let's just keep this between us for now."

I wasn't sure why Laura was so adamant about keeping this hushed, but I decided to not question her. "Fine," I replied. "I'll help you get to the bottom of this, but if I think it becomes important enough, I will use every source we have. Besides, I guess I have my own problem to deal with."

I was, of course, referring to this so-called prophecy deeming me the savior of the world, or at least the only chance the world has.

"Yeah." Laura sighed. We sat quietly for the next couple of minutes staring out the window, both of us clearly concentrating on the happenings of the past few days, attempting to discern all the things that had come to be revealed to us.

Eventually, Laura sighed and stood up, making her way to the far side of the room. She grabbed a towel off the rack next to the bathroom, and without saying another word, she stepped through the door and closed it behind her. I brought my hands together, interlocking the fingers, then fell straight back onto the bed.

My hands resting on my chest, I let my head fall to the left, and as I lay there peering out the half-covered window, I could feel my eyes growing heavy and as I resolved to let them remain closed, I quickly faded off to sleep.

* * *

Eddie and Camille had already picked up a map from a local shop and were well on their way to getting tickets on the next train headed to Chile. Camille's fluent Spanish and knowledge of the city were impressive, and Eddie was proud of his sister for taking charge of her life regardless of being held against her will by the cult and being forced to live on the run. He watched as she interacted with a local who she had paid to purchase four tickets in two trips from two separate ticketing booths.

When she was finished, she turned to Eddie and handed him the tickets. "See, easy peasy," she said with a smirk on her face.

He smiled at seeing his sister relaxed for the first time since their reunion. "It's good to have you back, Camille," he said to her.

"It's good to be back," she replied, staring back at him. She stood there for a moment, staring, before thrusting her arms around him. "I've missed you so much, Eddie," she said. As Camille hugged him, even Eddie couldn't hold in his emotions.

Only days before, his sister had been lost to him for ten years, she was never going to be back in his life, and now she was here in his arms. Eddie was silent, but his tears spoke for him. He held her tightly and swore to himself he would never let her out of his grasp again. "I'm sorry I wasn't there for you, Camille."

"Don't Eddie, there isn't a thing you could have done, and still, according to Laura, you and Ray spent a long time searching for me. I don't blame you for anything."

Eddie stayed silent. He just wanted to stay in this moment for as long as he could. "Eddie," she said.

"Yeah?"

"About this drinking. I'm sorry I drove you to it."

Eddie stepped back from his sister and wiped the tears from his face. "Yeah, about that." For the first time in his life, he felt ashamed of his drinking. "I was lost for a long time Cammie," he said, catching himself right as it was too late.

She glared at him for a moment, then smiled through her own tears. "It's OK, Eddie. You can call me that stupid nickname if you want to."

Eddie had taken to calling her that as a way of teasing her back when they were kids. 'Cammie, Cammie, where's your shammy' He would say whenever he felt like embarrassing her in front of her friends.

"I'll try to refrain," he said. "And about the drinking. I'll be giving it up. At least I think I will be." Eddie certainly wanted to give up drinking, and having his sister back should definitely give him enough drive to do so.

After all, he only began after his efforts at finding his sister had failed. He did, however, know all too well the addiction of his habit, and he knew a great deal of support would be needed, but he didn't think he'd even need to ask her to be there. So, he didn't. Instead, he just looked at her and smiled, again wiping away the tears from his face.

Camille said nothing further about the drinking. She stared at her brother and smiled. "Let's get back to the motel. These tickets are for a few hours from now, and we should probably get a little rest. Who knows when we're going to get another chance?"

Eddie smiled back at his sister and put his arm around her shoulder. "Sounds good to me," he said as they began to make their way away from the station. Eddie took one last look at the tickets, and as he was about to pocket them, he looked again. "Cammie, what's today?"

Chapter 9

"Eddie and Camille look like they've made amends," I said, looking over to Laura as she swayed slightly in the saddle of the Chilean Corralero. The hefty breed of horse local to Chile is said to be among the hardiest in all the world, and out here, in the arid Atacama Desert and rocky terrain of the Andes where they are most often used, I could see why.

"Yea, I see it too," she replied. The frustration of having to travel horse-back through the wilds of Chile instead of sitting comfortably in a train was clear in her voice, and while Camille and Eddie were riding up front with one of the guides, getting an idea of what the day's ride was going to be like, she and I were taking up the rear.

As it turned out, the tickets that Camille had purchased were a few days old. Apparently, the local that she paid to get the tickets had kept the money and gave her some old ones. This little act of foul play forced us instead to hire some hausos, or Chilean cowboys, to guide us from the border, through the Andes, and to an abandoned mining town known as Potrerillos.

Camille had heard mention of the town several times toward the end of her stay in Chile, but admittedly, she hadn't had the time to chase down any facts about the fairy tale.

There were several versions of the tale, but the one she relayed to us was about an old miner who had claimed to have once found a sword in the mines that was so cold that when he touched it, it froze his finger right off. When the miner tried to return with his fellow workers, he was unable to find the sword again.

Even though Camille hadn't managed to dig anything up during her stay, the extra day we had to spend preparing for our journey gave us time to do some digging of our own, and after discovering the nature of its closure, we decided Potrerillos was as good a place as any to start. The official report was that the quality of the oar was diminishing, but a local tabloid mentioned a body being found frozen solid just a year before it closed.

I watched Camille lean over to Eddie and say something. He then turned his horse and made his way back to us. I had never known Eddie to have ridden a horse before, but he certainly handled his steed as if he had been riding all his life.

"Camille says we're going to be entering the Atacama this evening, and then we'll make camp until morning. She also said tonight's going to be cold, and tomorrow is going to be really, really hot."

We had been on the trail for a few days, and Camille was the only one of us who wasn't showing any wear. "How does she do it?" Laura asked.

"My guess is ten years of living here," Eddie replied, smiling as he playfully circled us on his horse.

It was clear that having Camille back in his life was having a very profound effect on Eddie. A great deal of change was taking place in him, and I wasn't the only one to notice it.

For starters, there was his drinking. Eddie hadn't touched a drop since his sister's return, and aside from the initial glance at the bottle immediately following our return from the mansion, he hadn't even looked twice at a drink. He was also beginning to show signs of a man who has something to live for in his life. All around, my partner was starting to act like an ordinary, happy, cheerful man.

Laura and I shared a look as he squeezed himself and his horse between us. "You know, I always wondered what it would be like to ride a horse. It's pretty fun, yeah?"

Laura was the one to respond to his interrogative statement. "I grew up riding," she said. "And I never quite enjoyed it. Of course, my father was always pushing me to sit up straight and listen to my instructor, so that might have had something to do with it."

"Instructor?" I said inquisitively. "And why did you have to sit up straight?" I added.

"Oh, you know, my father thought it was a good idea for his daughter to learn to ride to showcase. So naturally, my posture was as important as the horse's."

"Yep, that would definitely take the fun out of it," Eddie replied. "Well, if you're up for a race sometime, we should have a go," he said, bending slightly forward, ready to give his horse a good tap to the sides with his heels.

"Oh, here," he said, tossing me a small brown leather-bound journal. I was on the verge of asking him what it was when I noticed the letter V burned into it. "Yeah, it's what you think," he said.

He finally gave his horse a kick while simultaneously shouting 'yaaa' and took back off toward his sister. "Racing isn't lady-like," Laura said, adjusting her posture.

"Are you sure that isn't your dad talking?" I said before giving my own horse a nudge while pocketing the journal. "Come on, Laura," I said. "Live a little."

I was curious about the journal, but Eddie's cheerfulness had rubbed off on me, and I was far more interested in just enjoying myself for the time being. Looking back, I watched Laura toss her eyes back and give an under-her-breath 'Oh screw it' before she too brought her horse to a trot to catch up to the rest of us.

* * *

I thumbed through the journal, taking a good deal of time to examine each entry with the care that it deserved. The handwriting was a thing of beauty, and the words were powerful and moving. "You know what," I said, looking across the fire to Eddie. "Even seeing it with my own eyes, I still can't believe that that beast was ever a good-looking, albeit eccentrically dressed woman."

Eddie looked over from across the fire. "Yeah," he said with a sigh. "You know, I know we were just trying to stay alive, but I do feel kind of bad about killing her."

"Hey, we didn't know," he reminded me. "Besides, from what my sister tells me, she wasn't exactly a saint."

"I know," I said, "but she didn't seem all that bad when she greeted us." Eddie went back to looking up at the stars, and I turned the page to read the next entry.

It wasn't easy keeping him a secret. Master Tamile has been questioning me for months now why I've prolonged my stay here in the northern camps. I can only hope that he takes me at my word and doesn't come snooping around. I suppose that even if he did, he wouldn't get much. The two men who accompanied me were pretty well fools, and it was easy enough to rid myself of them when the time came that they began to suspect I was pregnant—

I stopped reading and looked over at Eddie again. "Eddie, did you read any of this?" I asked.

"No," he replied without taking his eyes off the sky. "I was going to but decided it best to let you do the legwork." Hearing in his voice, the smirk that he was wearing at the comment, made me consider tossing the lizard that was resting on the rock next to the fire right into his lap. I decided against punishing the little guy for Eddie's annoying me, and I went back to reading.

Killing The big one was easy, but Jeff wasn't a half-bad guy. He was as stupid as most, but he was also somewhat nice to me. I wish he would have just looked the other way— I do feel some remorse for having killed him, but I couldn't let him tell the magister. If he found out that I bore a son, then he would be as much a prisoner to this world as I am.

"She felt like a prisoner," I mumbled.

"What's that?" Eddie said.

His attentiveness to the stars had faded, and he had grown more interested in why I was paying such close attention to the journal. "It appears Miss Valora wasn't the last Cynanthrope after all."

Deciding the information in the journal may be worth his time after all, Eddie got up from his position across the fire and moved to take a seat next to me. "It says here that she had a son, and looking forward, there may even be a few more of her kind."

"Go on then," Eddie said. "Read it." So I did.

Stanislav and his family have agreed to take the boy in. I can only hope that he is still up to the task of teaching him what it means to be a Cynanthrope. Without his guidance, I would have never made it as far as I did before that unfortunate evening when I was discovered by Monstre—If only I hadn't been such a fool. I guess that's why they say only fools love wholeheartedly.

I paused for a moment, thinking about what it must have been like to have your freedom taken from you under the guise of love.

"Well, keep reading then," Eddie nudged me, clearly intrigued by our would-have-been killer's past entanglement with romance. Eddie may have been the dictionary definition of a man's man, but he certainly was a sucker for a good tale of the heart. I let out a sigh and continued.

I thought Desmond to be a good man, kind and gentle, and understanding. I even felt safe when I was with him.

That, I suppose, had been my mistake. To think that someone like him could have ever loved someone like me—

I thought that our love was strong enough, that he would accept me for what I was or at the very least keep my secret to himself—I guess you never really know someone. I guess, at the worst, I just expected him to run away in terror and never come back, but I never would have thought that he was a member of the Monstre des Ténèbres. A Tracker bent on confirming the rumors about me.

Our love wasn't real. He used me, found me out, and then made me a slave to his cause. I could have killed him; his betrayal stung but back then, somewhere deep inside, I guess I still thought some of it had been real. I know now that it wasn't and wish I had taken his life just as he had taken mine—That I had stripped him of his dignity just as those he followed had done to me as they collared me and controlled me—That's why I had to kill Jeff. My son will never be a slave to these people.

"OK, now I feel bad too," Eddie said. "You don't suppose the boy is still alive, do you?" he asked.

I looked at him quizzically as if he should have known the answer. "Don't quote me on it, but I would venture to guess that Valora meant what she said about her son never being a slave. Chances are he's alive and well."

Eddie made a hmm sound before moving back to the other side of the fire. "It's getting late. We better save the rest of that for another time," he said.

I nodded in agreement, tucked the journal away in my saddlebag, and slouched back against the log I had propped myself up against.

Looking around the camp, I could see that the girls were already well into their slumber, and in all likelihood, Eddie wouldn't be far behind them. The hausos, too, were all lights out, which meant I was alone under an Atacama sky with only a half-baked lizard to keep me company.

"Well, what do you say, Bob?" I said, looking over at the cold-blooded creature warming himself on the boulder nearest the fire.

The little guy's eyes were closed. "I guess I should take that as a sign." I closed my eyes, and as I lay there, my thoughts drifting between the happenings of the past few days and the sounds of the desert, I couldn't help but feel like someone should be keeping watch. Perhaps it was just paranoia, or maybe it was just a result of watching so many westerns growing up where someone always took the first watch.

Regardless, I stirred at the thought, and in some random attempt to please my subconscious, I reached over and poked Bob. With one eye open, I saw him scurry to the top of his perch, now awake and fully alert. Somehow this made me feel better, and within minutes I faded off to sleep.

Chapter 10

When we roused from our sleep the following morning, I had been surprised to see Bob still perched on the boulder by the fire. He was wide awake, and for a moment, I wondered if he had kept watch the entire night.

Unfortunately, as had been the case with most of our journey, there was little time to think about such a trivial thing. The hausos had insisted that we get an early start, and it had only taken them a few minutes to pack up, saddle the horses, and scarf down a tin can of beans that one of them had managed to not only cook but dish out in that same time.

The crisp morning breeze had been a welcoming start to the second half of our journey, but the day had grown hot after the rising of the sun, and I was thankful to have been rushed out of my sleeping bag so early.

Unlike yesterday, there was no cheerful mood about any of us. The heat was having its way with us, and the rocky terrain had the horses stepping in a more or less stiff step, so there was no comfort to be found in the saddle. I watched as Eddie feigned a smile, and when his sister glanced over at him, I could see that even she wasn't immune to this kind of punishment.

Laura bobbed in her saddle, seemingly oblivious to the world around her. I could tell she was deeply concentrated on understanding what her role was in this adventure of ours, and that got me wondering if the distraction from the overwhelming heat was a welcomed one or if it was just as bad as suffering through the ride.

"Mmm." I groaned at the frustration of being coated in dust as we made our way across the vast desert, and while the heat had never really been an issue for me, even I was feeling the effects of the dry heat of the Atacama.

Needless to say, it wasn't too difficult to hide my excitement when we were finally able to make out the peaks of the Andes ahead of us. And yet, despite being in view of what was to be our haven from this unbearable heat, we still had a few hours ride to reach it, and I needed to find a way to distract myself.

I knew trying to make conversation wasn't the answer, so instead, I settled to distract myself in the same manner as Laura. My mind drifted to Hurston. Being the most recent of our encounters with the cult, it was fresh in my mind. Not to mention it was probably the most clear-cut event of the past few days. I'd known Hurston to come out of some tough situations before; the guy had a knack for getting himself into tight places, but a dragon.

This was different. Sure, I could recall a few times where Hurston had barely managed to escape some serious situation by the skin of his teeth, but if he had managed to make it through his dance with the dragon, I would never hear the end of it. Hell, if he'd made it out of there alive, I'd have to let him off the hook. I put the thought to rest, reminding myself that Hurston had luck on his side as much as his skill.

The thought faded, and I turned my attention to Eddie. While he was most definitely happy with his sister's return, I did wonder how their reunion would affect him in the long run. He was a good partner, but with his sister in the picture, I did wonder if I would lose him to her.

Ten years without her would certainly warrant him making a choice to stop working so that he could make up for lost time. Having no long-lost sibling myself meant that I could not relate to his situation, and as such I couldn't be sure what he would do; this made me feel uneasy.

Eddie and I were as close as partners could get, and it's safe to say that in all our time together, there had been very few times when either of us didn't know what the other was thinking. But this, this was one of those rare occasions where I was clueless about what was on his mind, and not knowing what he would do when this was all over bothered me.

I was sure that I would miss my partner if he decided to leave the Ray Shields Detective Agency, and I began to think of what I would say to him to convince him to stay. Then I realized how selfish my thoughts were and decided to focus on one puzzle at a time.

"Hmm," I let out a satirical gest of amusement as I began to think about what Camille had said back in my office. Her words echoed in my mind. 'A shield will stand against the darkness; sword in hand—you are that shield, Ray'.

The thought both amused and concerned me. How was I supposed to stop a creature made of magma and lightning that was so large that it was locked away under a volcano? And with a sword, nonetheless.

"Let's be real," I mumbled to myself. A magical sword of ice vs. a monster with a running temperature of fourteen hundred degrees Fahrenheit; one would think the ice would simply melt upon contact. Then again, the sword was made by a god, was it not? Perhaps I shouldn't be questioning the know-how of the gods. Maybe when struck, the molten monster would simply begin to solidify just like magma does when it spews out into the ocean.

Whatever the deal with the sword, the story that Camille told us about the miner who lost his finger and the tabloid article about a man found frozen solid had me worried. How was I even supposed to hold a sword so cold that it could freeze someone solid, let alone wield it against a force of great evil?

I shuttered at the thought of it all and came out of my head to see that we had already passed out of the desert and were well into the hill country. I looked over to see Eddie riding alongside me. "Hey, Eddie," I said. "How long have we been riding through these hills?"

"About three hours," he responded. "You looked preoccupied, so we all just left you be."

I looked around and realized that not only had my scenery changed but that it was no longer morning. It was well into the afternoon, perhaps pushing the evening, and the temperature was beginning to change. The thought that I had been on autopilot for three hours in these foothills and for several hours in the desert was concerning, but the truth was that this was without a doubt the strangest and most confusing case that ever crossed my desk. If one could call it a case at all.

"We should be getting close," Eddie said, handing me a canteen. Accepting it, I realized that either I hadn't drunk a thing for half the day or that whatever part of me that took over while I was in my head didn't want ol' Ray to die of dehydration and had probably emptied my canteen just as if I had been present for the rest of our trip through the desert. I reached for my canteen and confirmed that it was, in fact, empty.

"The hausos said this would be the most direct route," Eddie continued.

I looked around to see that our guides were no longer riding with us. "I suppose you sent them on their way."

"Actually," Eddie replied. "They were never going to take us all the way. The mine scares them."

"I don't blame them," I said, stirring in my saddle anxiously.

"It's just ahead," Camille said as she trotted back toward us. "The mine is just beyond that hill. We should be seeing it any minute now." Camille slowed her horse as she neared, maneuvering the mount alongside Eddie. "Laura rode ahead to get a look," she said.

As the three of us crested the hill, we came to look upon nearly a mile-and-a-half-wide complex. Two smokestacks loomed over the facility, and though there was no longer smoke pouring out from them, the years of use were apparent. Nearly one-third of the facility had been blackened from soot, making it easy to distinguish between the parts of Potrerillos that had been used for smelting ore and the now ghostlike town that once housed, entertained, and fed the miners.

Ahead, Laura was making her way into the facility without us. "The hell is she up to?" Eddie said.

"I don't know," I replied. "But we better catch up to her."

"It's not like her to be so reckless, Ray," he added.

He was right. It wasn't like Laura to do something so reckless, and here she was riding into a potentially dangerous situation, leaving what little safety there was in our numbers. Then it hit me. With her visions and the lack of control, she seemed to have while experiencing them, I began to wonder if she was even in control right now. I lost control myself, and without saying a word to the others, I let out a "yaa," giving my horse a hard kick.

I felt her front end slightly rise as every muscle tensed underneath me. She lunged forward, and while I had leaned in, the sheer power of this magnificent creature nearly tossed me from the saddle.

Leaning tighter, I steadied myself, and I began to feel the rhythm of her gallop underneath me. I let out a "Hu-ya," urging her forward. I could feel her pushing herself as her pace quickened to what was probably her last gear. It felt as if she could sense the desperation in me and knew that nothing else mattered but getting Laura.

Ahead, Laura was well into the town, and while I still had eyes on her, my gut told me she wasn't safe. We were closing fast, and it was all I could do to hang on and hope that nothing would happen to her. My heart raced, and as I watched her turn a corner, it went into overdrive. I had to reach her; I just had to.

Behind me, I could hear a faint holler of what sounded like Eddie yelling, but between the noise of my own horse sprinting across the desert and the noise inside my head, I couldn't make out what he said. Ignoring the call, I too made the corner that Laura had, and seeing that she was nowhere to be found, everything around me came to a sudden stop.

It was like time stopped, and I didn't. My horse was still. The ground beneath us was still. The smoke from the stack no longer lifted, and the cloud of dust I had left in my wake hung in the air, motionless. Nothing around me moved, and while this might have given me the slightest bit of hope that I would find Laura sitting atop her horse somewhere near me, that wasn't the case.

I must have turned in my saddle three or four times before I spotted her horse, riderless, tied to a post on a building that read Teatro Andes. Instinctively, I felt myself pulling on the reins of my own horse. The world around me rushed back to life, and though moments before I had been able to see everything in studied detail, the quickened pace let loose a rush of senses, and I suddenly felt sick and unable to make heads from tails.

My horse had come to a stop about fifty feet from the building, and I lurched out of my saddle and began to spill my breakfast all over the dry earth at my feet.

My horse neighed and backed away from the pile on the ground. If I hadn't still been holding the reins, she might have run off from disgust. Regaining my bearings, I looked up to see Eddie and Camille riding up. Together they slowed their horses, dismounted, and began walking toward me in what would have been an amusing moment of synchronization any other time.

"Where is Laura?" Camille asked.

I looked over at her horse and took note of how it had been tied to the post. Had anything happened to her, I doubt her horse would have been tied up. "I don't know," I replied between breaths. "Maybe she's inside."

I motioned to the building, and the three of us came to face it. In front of us were three separate doors. This wasn't surprising given that the building read Teatro Andes, which, when translated into English, means Andes Theater. We all looked at one another and pulled on a handle to the door in front of us.

It was dark inside, and while I could see the light beaming through the three doorways into the dark room, when I stepped in, letting the door close behind me, I realized that I was no longer standing alongside my partner or his sister.

I turned and tried to open the door. It was shut solid. I pushed against the door, repeatedly putting my shoulder into it before eventually giving up. Nothing that had happened in the past few days made any sense. Why should this be any different?

Reaching under my jacket, I pulled my Python from the holster and began to make my way through the small lobby. It was dark, but there was still enough light coming from a broken window to my left somewhere at the top of the wall.

While untouched by the element outside, the inside of the building hadn't fared any better than the outside. The counter that likely acted as a concession stand was rotten and nearly in a pile at the center of the room. Behind it, a few metal vents and a popcorn machine were all that remained of the workspace. At the far end of the room, a door labeled hombre hung on a single hinge. All around, the theater was an eerie mess.

It took a few minutes of fumbling in the dark to find the entrance to the auditorium. The doorway was hidden behind a curtain that I had mistaken for a tapestry, so I missed it the first time. Brushing the curtain aside, I entered the large hall, only to be faced with yet another puzzle.

Unlike the lobby, the large screening room was clean and orderly. Candles hung from the walls, lighting nearly every corner of the room and the seats, while clearly worn, were just as one would expect them to be. Other than an extravagant work of art muraling the ceiling, this was your average spend an evening out kind of theater. Well, minus the functioning lobby, that is.

"I've been expecting you," a hoarse voice said from down the aisle. I spun from my gawking position at the ceiling's fine craftsmanship to see a man dressed in a dark gray robe. His appearance matched that of the cultists described by Camille, and his demeanor and overconfident-like posture, even in facing the barrel of my .357, told me that this was not just another cultist but the magister himself.

"Mr. Bennings, I presume," I said, keeping my gun trained on him.

"In the flesh," he replied. "And you would be the great Ray Shields I've read so much about."

I thought about his comment for a moment. He said read about, not heard about. He smirked at his own statement, and I could see the worn expression of a man crazy with power. "In the flesh," I said mockingly.

The smirk on his face disappeared. "Be careful, Mr. Shields," he said. "Your life and those of your friends are in my hands." He gestured to the back of the hall.

Keeping my gun aimed in his direction, I turned and looked up to see Eddie and Camille staring at me through the small window of the projection room; behind them, a single man with long black hair. I was a little confused by the sight. Eddie easily had a foot on the man, and from what I could see of his slender physique, it didn't leave me with any impression that he was stronger than he looked.

I turned back to Allister. "What do you want?"

"Nothing from you," he said. "Her, on the other hand," Allister motioned toward Camille. "She has value to me, and I intend on taking her with me."

When I looked back at Eddie and his sister, I could tell by the look on his face that he could hear everything. His eyes were angry, and I could see that he wanted nothing more than to throttle the life out of Bennings himself, but behind the anger, I saw something I had rarely seen in my friend in all our years together; fear.

I turned my attention back to Bennings. "If you know so much about me, then you know I'm not going to just stand here idle and let you take one of my friends."

The cultist furrowed his brows in disappointment. "You're right. I guess I did know that," he said. He reached up and pulled from the neckline of his robe a long golden chain. When he reached the end, he held in his hand the medallion that had been in the photo delivered to my office.

From Camille's description of what had happened to the cultist who Allister had used this on, I knew the power of this thing, and the thought of what could come next scared me.

"It's much more powerful than that silly photo would have you believe." If he knew about the picture, he most certainly knew how it came to be in my possession. "Did you think I wasn't aware of Lewis's plan to try and stop me? I know everything that happens within my walls, Mr. Shields. I'm not as foolish as our last leader."

Slowly, he made his way down the aisle toward me. I was in the middle of telling him to stop when Allister mumbled something and then waved his hands. My arm grew heavy, and I began to find it difficult to keep my gun on target. I brought my other arm up to support the pistol, but soon the weight of the gun in my hands became too much, and I dropped it. I tried to bend and pick it up, but I found myself frozen in place.

"Now, I admire you, Ray," he said as he reached me. "Even more so, you've been stirring up all kinds of trouble for me, and I find your meddling to make this all the more fun." He positioned himself at my side and turned toward the stage. "I don't expect you to stop trying to put a halt to my plans. In fact, I look forward to it. But just so you know what you're up against, let me leave you with a little demonstration of my power."

He waved his hand at the stage, and the screen that hung at the front of the hall lifted away. Behind it, kneeling beside a slouched body on the ground, was a woman dressed in the same robes as Allister. The other figure was trying to stand up but couldn't seem to do so on his own.

He looked up. I was staring at Lewis, the man who had saved my life in the park and at the mansion. At least it appeared to be Lewis. His face was bloody and bruised, but that wasn't the reason why he couldn't stand. His legs appeared to be joined together as if sewn or melded.

"What have you done to him?" I exclaimed.

"Nothing compared to what I'm about to do to him or what I will do to you if you persist in trying to stop me."

Allister raised the medallion in his hand and began to chant. "Sko-Lagh eelantra Su-aman sal-etan."

The earth began to tremble at our feet, and beams of light began to burst through cracks in the stage surrounding Lewis and the woman. Though I couldn't be sure, I presumed her to be Ms. Patricia Valentine, Lewis's accomplice.

"Please. No!" the woman whimpered, tears in her eyes. Allister ignored her and repeated himself. The cracks began to widen, suddenly tearing a hole beneath the two cultists. Fire and smoke billowed from the hole, and for a moment, I thought I could hear the woman let out a scream that was halted short of being finished. The hole closed as fast as it opened, and the stage returned to normal.

"This is what happens to those who oppose me, Ray," Allister said. He walked back over to the stage and held his hand out to catch a piece of ash that fell slowly from the air. He closed his hand as if crushing the last piece of his enemy and turned back to me with a look of satisfaction.

"I hope you can see how powerless you are against me, Ray," Allister said, making his way back over to me. He stopped alongside me, and for a second, I thought of grabbing the medallion and wiping that smirk off his face with it, but that action never happened. I wanted to move, but I couldn't.

"You bastard," I said. At least I could still tell the guy off. "If you think any of this scares me, you better think twice."

While everything that had happened in the past few days was enough to make a man insane with fear, I was far too worried about Laura at the moment to be scared. "Laura," I said in a low voice. In all this time, he hadn't mentioned a word about her. For a moment, I thought of asking what he'd done with her, but if he didn't know she was even here, I'd only be putting her in danger.

"You underestimate me, Bennings." I blurted out. "Go ahead, keep sending your little pets after me, and I'll be sure to send you a postcard every time I kill one of them." The smirk on his face disappeared for a moment, and he furrowed his brow. "That get your attention?" I said.

He glared at me and then leaned in close. "You may have killed Valora and—" He paused for a moment, the irritation in his voice clear. "—amazingly escaped the clutches of my dragon, but, shield or no, you are nothing to me, and when I complete my master's bidding, nothing, not even you, will stand in my way."

He stepped back away from me and then barked an order at another cultist who had entered the room. "Toss them in the mine," he said. "A shield against the darkness," he said, scoffing at his twisting of the prophecy's words. I watched as he made his way back to the stage before a hood came down over my head and something hard hit me in the back of the head. Something really hard.

Chapter 11

I've only ever been knocked unconscious twice before, once in a bar fight that Eddie started and thankfully finished, and again last week following the exploding Valora. It goes without saying that the experience of waking from such a state leaves a person confused and if hit hard enough, feeling like the world has decided to put an end to their miserable life by squeezing their brains out.

My head hurt tremendously. I can only describe the feeling as being a cross between being unable to pop your ears, only inside your skull, and a throbbing so intense that it's enough to make a person want to vomit. Had I not emptied the contents of my stomach already, I would have done just that.

It was dark wherever I was, and the only sound I could make out was a dripping that came from somewhere to my left. Wherever I was, it was cold, dark, and apparently wet. The dripping melody was soon joined by a faint shuffling sound from somewhere on the other side of me, and for a moment, I was content sitting there in the dark, the pain in my head dulling with each drop of the water. Then I thought about the shuffling and how unnatural it was.

I bolted to my feet and backed away from the nearing sound. "Who's there?" I said, reaching for my gun. Only when my hand came to rest on the butt of the Colt did a sense of confusion set in. Why would they have given me back my gun?

"Ray, it's me, Eddie," I heard a voice say.

"Jesus, Eddie, you nearly gave me a heart attack," I replied.

"Sorry," he said. "It's just so dark in here, and I didn't want to go walking off a ledge or something, so I've just been keeping my hand on the wall and sweeping my feet in front of me as I walk."

"Damn," I mumbled. In my haste to get up, I hadn't thought about keeping track of the wall, and now I stood in the darkness at least five feet from where I was with no way of being sure where the wall was.

It was almost like Eddie could read my mind. "Wall's over here, boss," he said reassuringly.

I made my way toward him cautiously, my arm extended and my feet shuffling. When I finally made contact with the wall, I noticed how jagged the surface was. It was cold, uneven, and rough. "How much have you been able to learn about where we are?" I asked.

"Not much," he said. "They put a hood over my head before tossing me in here, so I'm not even sure where here is." I nodded before realizing that he couldn't see I was acknowledging him. He continued anyway. "I know there is some sort of heavy iron door behind me, and I don't think there is any way of getting through it. Besides that, the dripping over that direction sounds a little far off, and these walls feel more natural than man-made. My guess is we're in some sort of cave or tunnel."

"What about your gun?" I asked.

"Gone," he said. "Yours?"

"Right here," I told him, pulling it free from its holster before turning the cylinder to see if it was loaded by way of feeling for cartridges. "It's loaded too, and the cartridges don't feel spent."

"What? Why would they give you your gun back?"

"I don't know," I said. "But it's a little unnerving." I could tell his being unarmed while I was fully loaded bothered him, and I decided to keep the conversation moving.

"What about Camille? Do you know where they took her?"

He was quiet for a moment. "No, I don't." The frustration in his voice deepened. "We need to get out of here, Ray. I can't lose her again."

"I know," I said. I wanted to comfort my friend, but I could say nothing that would do that right now. The truth of it all was that we were trapped in total darkness and had no way of telling where we were.

We stood quietly in the dark for the next few minutes. Neither of us said a word, and I was just beginning to wonder about Laura when Eddie spoke up. "Ray, I need one of your bullets and your gun."

Pulling my gun free of its holster, I emptied the cylinder of all but one of the cartridges and handed it to him. "What are you planning?"

When he didn't say anything, I simply leaned back against the wall and waited. It's not uncommon for Eddie to ignore others when he's concentrating. In fact, it's likely so frequent an occurrence that I've grown accustomed to the silent moments spent in waiting.

The smell of whiskey hit my nose and, when I heard the sound of something tearing, I realized what he was up to. "You know, Eddie," I said. "I would have taken the bullet out of the casing for you."

He remained silent and kept working. After about a minute, he spoke up. "I got a bit of my sleeve dowsed in, Jack," he said. "And I put a little of the powder on it as well. I'm gonna shoot with just the casing and primer now. Are you ready?" he asked.

"Yeah, go ahead," I replied.

Perhaps it was because I was surrounded by complete darkness, or maybe it was just because I wasn't the one pulling the trigger, but even though I was expecting the sound of the primer going off, I still jumped when it did. The popping sound was likely amplified by our being in a tunnel, and the fireball that followed the pop of the primer being fired was quite the display when it ignited Eddie's tightly wound, alcohol-soaked sleeve.

He had stuffed it in one end of his holster, which he now held in his hand. "It was the best I could do," he said when our eyes finally met. "I'm just glad you still had that tin on you."

"Yeah," he muttered before holding the holster up and looking around. "Thank Cammie," he said. "It was her idea that I keep it in my jacket. Something about how the weight of it would help me make it through the day without thinking about needing a drink."

While the idea of an alcoholic who was trying to stop drinking, carrying a tin full of whiskey in his jacket seemed counterproductive to me, the more I thought about it, I could see how maybe carrying an empty one in his pocket might somehow work on a subconscious level.

"I'll be sure to do that when we get out of here," I said.

Eddie lifted the holster and held it out in front of him as he walked past me. The light from his makeshift torch was enough to reach both sides of the fifteen-foot-wide tunnel, and I could see that the ceiling was just above Eddie's head in some areas and couldn't have been more than seven feet tall at its highest point.

It was clear that we were in an old part of the mine. The floor was simply dirt, and the walls, while clearly cut by some kind of heavy-duty boring machine, were rough and looked like they were made decades ago.

It was silent between us for the next half hour or so as we made our way in the direction of the dripping. By the time we finally found the source, Eddie's long-sleeve torch was nearly extinguished. We stopped, and it was my turn to sacrifice a part of my wardrobe to be burned. Eddie wound my sleeve tightly while I poured whiskey on it.

As he finished placing the new torch head in his holster, using the last of the old flame to ignite it, we heard a familiar sound from ahead of us. "Scraaac." Eddie lifted the torch to see that we were standing ten feet from the source of the dripping and another three feet from our gargoyle friend that had helped us escape the cultists' mansion. The water was puddling near its feet, dripping from a tilted mining cart that had been collecting water for who knows how long.

"Scraaac." The creature sounded off again before plunging its face down into the water in what must have been an act of drinking. When it raised its head to see Eddie and me just standing there, it looked confused. It stood back up and made a low, grunting sound.

"Easy there, fella," Eddie said. "I ain't thirsty, but I could use a little something to wash up with." Eddie handed me the torch and made his way over to the water. Kneeling, he dipped his whole head in the water, then after nearly ten seconds, he whipped his head back and ran his hand over and through his hair. The creature looked pleased for a moment, mimicking Eddie's movements with his own hand before putting his fist out to Eddie.

"Would you look at that?" Eddie said, bumping fists with the gargoyle. "He likes me."

"Yeah," I replied. "Kindred spirits."

"So, what do we call you?" Eddie asked from his still kneeling position. The creature tilted its head as if a little confused. "I'm Eddie," Eddie said, holding his hand to his chest, following with, "That's Ray."

"Scraaac," the creature screeched as he looked back and forth between Eddie and me before a look of understanding crossed its face. It then brought its hand up and lay its claws across its own chest. Then it let out a long "Scraaaaaac." Eddie and I looked at each other for a moment, then back to the gargoyle.

"We'll figure out what to call you later," Eddie said. The small gargoyle tilted his head a little but didn't seem to take offense. "Have you seen my sister?" Eddie asked.

The gargoyle didn't respond. Eddie put his hand to his chest and then ran his hands along the side of his head, mimicking the presence of longer hair.

"My sister," he said again to the creature. The gargoyle's eyes widened before letting out another of its screeching sounds. He raised his hand and beckoned for us to follow. Eddie finished ringing the water from his hair as I handed him the torch, and I began to regret not dunking my head as well.

"Finally, things are looking up," he said, nudging me with his shoulder.

"Yeah, let's hope it stays that way," I replied, and the two of us followed our guardian gargoyle deeper into the mines.

* * *

The walls of the mine shaft passed slowly. Laura sighed, leaning against the cage, and began toying with the switches on the panel to her right. The elevator continued its long, slow descent, and she gave up on her attempt to reverse course. She was lost, separated from Ray and the others, and had no clue how she came to be here.

The last thing she remembered was talking with Eddie's sister. Everything after that was a blur. One minute she was on her horse, keeping a slow, steady pace, waiting for the others to catch up, and the next, she was closing the door of this relatively small cage, locking herself inside an elevator that seemed to go in only one direction; down.

She had no doubt that the how of her current state was attributed to her visions and lack of control thereof, but there had been no vision this time. She was in one place, then another, with no recollection of the in-between. She began to wonder how long she had been in that tiny cage when the squealing of the cable faded, and the elevator slowed to a stop at the base of the shaft.

Opening the doors, she stepped out, letting the cage door slam shut behind her. The lights inside the elevator turned off, and for a moment, she found herself standing alone in the dark.

The light inside the cage flickered and came back on as the cable began to once again squeal under the weight of the elevator, and it began to lift away.

From what little light the single bulb produced, Laura was able to determine that she was standing at the entrance to a long corridor with stone walls. She was certain she was in the mine but had no idea how she would get out. Squinting, she could barely make out what appeared to be a string of lights adorning the walls, and she set to looking for any kind of switch before the light of the elevator dimmed, leaving her in the darkness with no chance of escape.

She found a lever on the wall near the elevator shaft and pulled it.

"Here's to hoping," she said as she waited for some kind of result. There was none. She nearly panicked, and she began to toggle the lever on and off rapidly before realizing there was a second lever right next to the one that she had her hand on. Flipping the second lever immediately rendered the desired result and the tunnel ahead of her lit up.

She stared down the long narrow corridor and considered her options. The chances of her getting the elevator to come back down were slim, and besides, she still needed to find the sword and, more importantly, her companions. She saw no other choice and began her trek into the mine.

Chapter 12

Eddie and I followed our newfound friend closely, stopping only twice to renew our makeshift light source. Eddie's poor holster was at the end of its life when we lucked out and found the butt of an old pickaxe that we happily converted into a new torch handle.

Eventually, we came to a junction in the tunnel where the path narrowed, and we were forced to choose between darkness and more darkness. Neither of these options seemed to bother Scarr, though.

Eddie had taken to calling him this after a failed attempt to get the creature to say his own name. Every word that left the gargoyle's mouth, in one way or another, resembled that word. He led the way, and as we followed, I realized that any reservations I may have had about the little guy were disappearing while Eddie's fondness for him only seemed to grow.

Eddie and Scarr were about eight or so steps in front of me when the ground let out an unsettling tremble. We stood motionless, waiting for the cave-in that was sure to follow; nothing. "Any chance we're close to getting out of here?" Eddie asked.

His question was directed at Scarr, and in the dim light cast off by the torch, his stout shoulders almost appeared to shrug. "Scarrc." Scarr's shriek echoed wildly down the corridor, and again we all stood waiting for everything to come crashing in.

When it was apparent that our choice of paths was, in fact, sturdier than we were imagining it to be, we continued on our way. Eddie and Scarr once again took the lead, and I trailed behind, listening for even the faintest sound that might indicate life inside this silent maze.

Occasionally, Scarr would come to a stop, beckoning us to do the same by raising his tail in a way that blocked any movement past him. Each time, he would slightly tilt his head and twitch his ears as if he were able to hear far beyond Eddie and me before taking a deep breath through the slots on his face that were undoubtedly his nostrils. Unaware of how the senses of a gargoyle worked, Eddie and I simply waited for Scarr to drop his tail before carrying on.

On the last of these stops, Scarr seemed to take longer than before, and it wasn't too long before Eddie and I thought that we could make out the faint sound of someone talking. It was low, real low, no louder than the tiniest whisper imaginable, but it was there.

Scarr seemed to hesitate for a moment, then he gave Eddie a curious smile before leaping to the ceiling, where he latched on and resumed a steady pace in the direction of the sound. Eddie and I exchanged glances, then continued our own pace following Scarr.

Within the first few minutes, the talking had grown louder, and we could tell that it was a single-sided conversation. Another minute passed, and our pace quickened as Eddie and I nearly simultaneously realized that the frustrated words of our guiding voice carried with it the hint of an accent.

Together we raced down the winding tunnel, both of us committed to reaching Laura first. Her voice grew louder as we grew closer, and the tunnel itself began to look brighter. We were starting to be able to make out more and more of the tunnel as we rounded each bend, and we could now see that this tunnel was lit, albeit dimly, by a trail of lights running along the wall. We made one last long bend in our race to Laura before coming to a halt.

If my heart didn't stop, my world certainly did. Laura, with all her elegance and determination, stood twenty or so feet from us, poised, ready to strike.

In one hand, she held firm the handle of a tool much like the one Eddie and I had used for our torch, and in the other, she aimed the deadly end of her blued Walther PPK. It didn't take but a second for her to realize that her would-be attackers were actually her closest friends. She lowered the gun, dropped her bludgeon, and ran toward us.

"Thank the heavens you guys are all right," she said as she thrust her arms around her two panting companions. The tenseness in her voice was gone, replaced only with a soft tone of relief. "I don't even know what happened," she continued, taking a step back. "One second, I was talking to Cami an—"

Her voice trailed off as she realized that only two of her companions stood in front of her. "—wait—" she paused, peering behind us as if expecting Camille to be bringing up the rear. When she saw that she wasn't, she finished her question. "—where's Camille?" she said, looking first at me and then at Eddie.

The softness that was present in her relief faded with the expression on Eddie's face, and it was all she could do to lean herself against the wall, bowing her head. "This is all my fault, isn't it?"

I reached out to comfort her when a sound that resembled that of a rock rolling across a stone floor came echoing from behind before making an abrupt thudding sound; Scarr had arrived.

Laura snapped to a fire-ready position with her pistol still in hand and probably would have pulled the trigger were it not for Eddie, who was already mid-fist bump with Scar. She lowered her gun. "I don't even want to know," she said, returning to her leaning position on the wall.

"Laura," I said, turning back toward her. "Everything is going to be OK. None of this is your fault."

"Yeah, L, don't worry, we're gonna find Cami yet." Eddie reserved calling Laura L for when he knew she was really upset or when he really wanted to suck up to her. He believed that nicknames disarmed people or, at the very least, took them off the edge. Still, his confidence in finding his sister did seem beyond what I expected it would be.

Perhaps the thought of losing his sister all over again would have been too much for him, or maybe her reappearance in his life simply brought back to life the more positive-minded Eddie that had walked through my doors all those years ago. Whatever the case, I was glad about it. Eddie was sharper and more focused than ever, and if the group had any chance of making it out of here intact, it needed to stay that way.

"Scarr here has been helping us find our way out," I said, tossing a thumb over my shoulder to the small gargoyle. "Well, at least he helped us find you," I continued, reaching my hand out, placing it on her shoulder. Laura lifted her head to look at me, and just as our eyes met, the hair on the back of my neck stood on end, and the two of us were thrust from our place in the tunnel.

Everything about where we were seemed to be the same, only the wall in which Laura had been leaning was now gone, replaced by a naturally but well-shaped door frame cut into the stone. I spun around nearly three or four times looking for Eddie and Scarr, but they were nowhere to be found.

"Eddie," I yelled. There was no answer.

"Ray." I looked over to see Laura pointing in the direction of the new tunnel. There was a strange blue luminous glow coming from somewhere on the other side of the opening.

"What now?" I said more generally than thoughtful, my focus still on where Eddie and Scarr had gone.

"I don't know," she replied, "but I think we should check it out." She paused, taking in a deep breath. "I think we need to check it out."

Without hesitation, she grabbed my hand with her free one, raised her PPK to the ready, and began leading us down the new tunnel. I didn't resist her tugging, though I did look back as if to make sure that our entrance could still be our exit, and possibly in an attempt to assure my mind that my eyes had been playing tricks on me and that Eddie and Scarr were in fact, still standing right there. They were not.

This tunnel, unlike the others, was short, and it didn't take long for us to find the source of the light. We stepped out from the tunnel and found ourselves standing in a large cavern staring up at a very big, very blue crystal. It was an astonishing sight, to say the least.

The crystal itself was at least fifty feet tall and probably measured four or five arm's lengths in diameter. It was definitely the source of the glow that had caught our attention, and while I knew little to nothing about geology or luminescence, to my knowledge, crystals didn't just glow, so the reason why this one was, left me curious.

Laura let go of my hand and began circling the curiosity. She made it about halfway around the crystal before stopping.

"What is it?" I said, attempting to make sense of the dismay that was now showing on her face. She didn't say anything. Instead, she just raised her hand and reached out for the crystal. I wanted to move to stop her. I wanted to tell her not to touch it. But for some reason, I was unable to do either. I just stood there and watched as Laura pressed the palm of her hand against the enormous crystal.

I watched as the smooth surface of the crystal lost its haziness, taking on the clear, delicate appearance of glass. It began to glow brighter and brighter until it was near impossible to look at, and as I began to back away, shielding my face with my hand, I was almost certain that I could make out the curvy silhouette of a woman standing inside of the massive glowing rock.

Lowering my hand, I squinted to confirm my suspicion when the whole thing began to vibrate and form tiny cracks that started spiderwebbing their way across the stone's clear surface. And then, with all the warning it could give, it suddenly shattered into thousands of tiny pieces.

I raised my arms to protect against the blast, expecting this to be the one that finally got me, but I felt nothing. Unlike the explosion back at the mansion where the concussion had been enough to throw me up a flight of stairs and through a door, the shattered crystal simply disintegrated into thin air.

Fragments of tiny luminous dust floated all around the cave, and as I recovered from my protective posture, I looked up to see Laura standing right where she was when she reached out to touch the crystal. The crystal, of course, was gone now, but levitating upright in its place was a large, glowing sword.

The blade was as white as arctic ice and had a deep, penetrating, blue hue that ran the length of the long double-edged blade, and the magnificently carved hilt was a dark royal blue with what appeared to be a giant serpent wrapping around it in just the right places to give the wielder a firm two-handed grip. A cool mist that seemingly emitted from the sword surrounded the weapon, and as the suspended blade continued to rotate, it glinted as if it were a single diamond with a thousand lights shining on it.

"Laura," I called to her, attempting to gain her attention. "Are you OK?" I asked.

She gave no response. Instead, she just stood there, her hand extended, palm out, with this look on her face that was distant and cold. That's when I noticed that her skin had also paled. I rushed toward her, continuing to call her name. "Laura, Laura, answer me," I said, putting my hands on her shoulders.

She was as cold as the sword looked. I pulled her and hugged her body to mine, attempting to warm her and bring her back to me. "Laura, don't you dare leave me!"

"Calm down, Ray," she said. I leaned back to look her in the eye, my grip on her shoulders still firm, and I was surprised to see that she had returned to her normal self. Her skin was no longer pale and cold, and that distant stare had disappeared and been replaced with Laura's naturally disarming eyes.

"I'm fine, Ray," she said reassuringly, before looking down at my hands on her shoulders. "Oh, right," I said, quickly removing them.

I stepped aside, hesitant to look away from her but eventually conceded, and we stood there together staring at the wonder in front of us. "Ray," Laura said, placing her hand on my cheek and turning my head to face her. "Ray, I know this is going to sound crazy, but I think this is meant for you."

"For me," I retorted. "Don't be so surprised, Ray," Laura said calmly, looking back at the sword. "A shield will stand against the darkness, sword in hand," she said, recalling the part of the prophecy that Camille connected to me.

She raised her hand, fingers extended, and sort of brushed the mist surrounding the sword with a curious smile on her face. She then turned to me. "Ray, you need to take the sword."

I looked at her, then at the sword, then brought my attention back to her. "Are you crazy?" I said. "Do you remember what supposedly happened to the miner who touched it?"

Laura's smile broadened in amusement, and she reached back for the sword, "Fine, if you don't do it, I will."

"No!" I yelled, reaching out to stop her.

She quickly moved her hand away from my grasp, causing me to overextend, placing my hand inside the protective mist surrounding the sword. The displaced cloud swirled around my wrist and down my arm like a snake, stopping only when it reached my shoulder.

I looked at Laura, bewildered at what was happening, but her eyes were calm and somehow reassuring. I turned my attention back on the sword, took a deep breath, then, for reasons unknown to me, reached the rest of the way out and wrapped my fingers around the hilt of the sword.

The mist hastened its circular path around my arm, spinning faster and faster until I could no longer make out the singular cloud that had snaked its way along my arm. The sword, frozen in my grasp, surged to life with cold continuous waves of air that burst in all directions.

Nervously, I looked over at Laura, who stood smiling, seemingly unaffected by the currents of cold air being released. She was calm, her posture unwavering in the face of this unknown. "Aggghhhh," I groaned in pain and tossed my head back as the cloud began constricting my arm.

"Just accept it, Ray," she said, placing her hand on my shoulder, it too unaffected by the swirling cloud of frozen mist.

Her touch filled me with an indescribable well of strength, and as I reached up and took hold of the rest of the hilt with my other hand, she stepped away. The pain intensified, and only when I stopped struggling to free myself did it subside. Both arms were now completely enveloped in the ice-cold cyclone, and as the sword began to shimmer, the mist began to slow and fade, and in the case of my right arm, sink slowly into my skin.

A powerful swell of energy rushed through me, and with all my might, and perhaps a large amount of borrowed energy, I thrust my arms forward and up, ripping free the sword from its levitating prison. One final shockwave of cold electrifying energy blew through the room before imploding back into the sword and then into me, and then all was still.

For a moment, I just stood there, the sword high above my head, firmly held in both hands, my mind racing to make sense of what just happened. I had never felt anything like it before. The raw power that poured through me when I grabbed the sword, the uncontrollable urge to hold on regardless of my will to let go, Laura's confidence in me to grab the sword and not freeze solid. It was all an overwhelming amount to process.

I snapped to and realized that I was breathing rather heavily when I heard Eddie's voice coming from just inside the tunnel.

"This way." He was shouting just as he entered the cavern to see me standing in what had to be the most ridiculous stance imaginable. That is, unless you had personally witnessed the accounts of the last few minutes.

"You uh—have the power, boss?" he asked, with his usual bit of sarcastic humor.

I retracted the sword and removed myself from my almighty stance before responding. "Actually, yeah, I think I do," I said, as the two of them came closer to examine the blade.

Eddie was about to touch it when he reconsidered. "Is it safe?" he asked.

I honestly had no idea, and I was about to tell him when Laura walked over. "Don't worry, it's fine," she said, running her hand gently along the edge of the blade down to the hilt. "But right now, I think we should be more focused on getting out of here. What do you think?" Laura lifted her hand and pointed toward the other side of the cavern.

I looked at her for a moment, still uncertain as to what had changed in her. She still sounded like herself, and she certainly didn't look any different, but something about her was off. I followed the direction of her finger to see an opening on the other side of the cavern. If this new tunnel had been there before we blew up a giant crystal and set loose a torrent of cold tsunami-like winds, I hadn't noticed.

Then again, I wasn't altogether sure how Eddie and Scarr even found us. One second, we were together, then we weren't. There was so much to make sense of, but Laura was right; getting out of here took priority. "Well, let's hope this one leads us out of here," I said, forcing myself to focus on the problem at hand.

I eased my grip on the sword a little and let it fall to my side before making my way toward what I hoped would be our way out of here when I heard Eddie cheerfully step up beside me. "Say, boss, that's a really cool-looking Tattoo you got there. When'd you get it?"

Chapter 13

His fate is in her hands. Laura thought to herself as she recalled the moment that she placed the palm of her hand against the giant crystal. She couldn't piece together what it was that possessed her to reach out so carelessly or even what it was that made her grab Ray's hand and rush into the room.

At the time, it was like someone else entirely was controlling her, and she was simply along for the ride. She still wasn't sure what was wrong with her, but she did feel more at peace than she could ever remember.

Something happened when she touched that crystal, and she knew it. It was like some part of her had been missing for so long, and from the moment she caused that sword to erupt from the crystal, she could feel that piece returning to her.

She pulled her canteen free from her horse's saddlebag and took a drink. Ray and Eddie were still looking for their horses, and Scarr was soaring high under the darkness of night, scouring the mining complex for any sign of the cult or Camille.

It was odd being out under the night's sky again. Wandering the darkness of the mine, even if only for several hours, had made her feel as if she hadn't seen the sky for days, and while it had not been as easy as making their way along a lighted four ft wide tunnel, they were out, and she was thankful for it.

The tunnel that appeared following Ray's retrieval of the sword was unlit and narrow. Still, between Scarr's ability to navigate in the dark and Eddie's willingness to give up the bottom half of both pant legs and the last of his Jack Daniels, the four of them managed to find themselves standing at the edge of the complex near what probably once served as a brothel.

Tucking her canteen back in its place, she pulled tight the strap holding down the flap of the saddlebag and turned around to look for any sign of Scarr. It was an odd thing getting used to.

After all, gargoyles were supposed to be a thing of myth and medieval architecture, not living, breathing creatures that gave fist bumps and took orders from a pair of private detectives. But here she was, waiting for Ray and Eddie to return and keeping her eye on the sky to see if Eddie's new friend would return or not. Eddie and Scarr seemed to really hit it off.

Ever since they began making their way out of the mines, Eddie and Scarr were joined at the hip. Scarr would look at Eddie, and he would say something like, "We're gonna turn here" or "Exits just up ahead." It's like the two had developed some unspoken way of communicating.

Whatever was going on, she was happy to see Eddie this way. He had always been a good man, but Laura knew something significant was missing from his life, and with Camille's return, so too returned that bit of him that had been locked away.

Now, with Camille missing, she was worried about him. Eddie was an expert at hiding his fear, but she knew he was scared. If anything were to happen to his sister, Eddie might never crawl out of whatever hole he would have found to hide in. It would be his grave.

The sound of her horse shuffling uneasily disturbed her thoughts, and Laura looked up to see Scarr swoop in and land hard atop a nearby boulder. His movements were swift and controlled, and there wasn't a doubt in her mind that he was a master of the sky.

Scarr stood atop the boulder motioning for her to get on her horse, and it wasn't until she answered him that she realized how easy it had been to understand what he was asking her to do. "What about the others?" she said, making her way over to her horse.

Scarr gave a nod, and while this could have meant any number of things, Laura could see in his eyes that he had understood her and was likely suggesting that he would be taking her to them. "Right," she said softly as she mounted her horse.

Pulling on the rains, she turned her steed toward Scarr. "Well, lead on." The four-foot gargoyle leaped high into the air, spiraling upward before falling back where he spread his wings and took off at a controlled pace down the street. He landed on the roof of a building down the road and looked back at her in wait. "Showoff."

Laura nudged her horse forward, settling into the saddle and the sway of the horse beneath her. "You and Eddie definitely have a lot in common."

*　*　*

Eddie and I watched as the cultists hurried to load the train. Whatever it was they were loading, there was a lot of it, crate after crate, and while I had it in mind to figure out a way to sabotage their progress, finding Camille took priority.

Eddie and I had been trying to locate our horses when Scarr swooped in excitedly, pointing and beckoning for us to follow. The result had us outside a large loading station for trains with cultists actively moving cargo and a few large creature-filled cages aboard one. We spotted our horses being led aboard as well, and Eddie just couldn't help but point out the obvious. "So much for getting the horses."

Eddie's morale was still intact, but I could tell that it was fading with every passing moment that his sister's whereabouts went unknown.

"And I was just thinking we could smuggle 'em back with us," I said, nudging my partner. Eddie nodded, his focus on one cultist in particular. He wasn't very big and was dressed in the same gray robes as all of his fellow cultists. He couldn't have been more than eighteen, was as scrawny as they came, and the only thing unique about him was the blue instead of green sash he wore to keep his robes closed.

"You got some kind of date with the kid over there," I said.

"That—" Eddie paused briefly. "—Kid over there is the arrogant little shit that took my gun." Eddie calmly clenched and unclenched his jaw a couple of times before continuing. "I intend on getting it back, and when I do, I'm gonna teach that boy a lesson."

I hadn't been there to know what took place before Eddie was thrown into the mines, but whatever it was, he had it in for this kid, and I kind of felt sorry for the lad.

I was about to suggest that we get a closer look when I heard Scarr and Laura approaching from behind us. "Glad to see that Scarr understood what I meant by bring Laura here," I said, watching her dismount from her horse.

"Yeah," Eddie prodded. "We were almost certain that he would just swoop you up and fly back here with you kicking and screaming the whole way."

"Scaarcac," Scarr let out what almost sounded like a chuckled version of his screech.

The three of us looked at him and let out hushed laughter of our own. "Well, as you can see, he let me come of my own volition, which is only half the reason why we took so long."

She approached and took a knee beside us. When she saw the train and its passengers, she instinctively lowered her voice, though it was hardly necessary at this distance.

"We ran into a group of those cultists on our way here and had to double back and go around them. I also overheard them say that Bennings was planning something for their new guest." She made air quotations with the remark and continued. "They also said she was already on board. I guess that means the train."

I half expected Eddie to march straight down to the train, provide the kid with a fistful of education, collect his gun, and take on the entire cult. Instead, he looked to Scarr, who, in seeing Eddie's look of determination, nodded before leaping high into the air in nearly the same fashion as we had seen him do before.

"He may be short, but he still has ups," Eddie said as the gargoyle's dark olive-green skin melted into the night sky.

Chapter 14

It was hard to keep track of Scarr as he glided skillfully across the moonless sky. Occasionally we would catch a glimpse of him, or at least what we thought was him, before once again finding ourselves staring in wonder. Eventually, we saw him landing atop a car somewhere in the middle of the train's long convoy of boxcars and passenger coaches.

We watched as he crept skillfully across the top of the train. His wings were tucked sharply at his side as he made his way forward, and for just a second, I almost thought I could see him smile. I don't know the pastimes of gargoyles, but he seemed to be exceedingly pleased even after his initial return from scouting. At the time, I thought perhaps he was just happy to lend a hand, but now, I wasn't so sure that was the case.

After Scarr's little scouting expedition, it was decided that Eddie, Laura, and I would position ourselves ahead of the last car by a few hundred yards and wait until it came within reach to spring for the caboose. We still had no idea where we would find Camille on the train, but it was clear that we needed to work in one direction, lest we run the chance of missing her entirely.

That plan, of course, as with most of our plans this trip, had to be scratched when we saw Allister entering at the front of the train.

We couldn't risk letting Allister use that amulet again. It was definitely powerful, and while I never would have believed that a necklace had magical powers that could be used for a range of destructive things. Everything from controlling its victim's actions to opening a portal to hell and incinerating them.

I also would have never believed in dragons or dog people, or that a magical sword of ice used to imprison an evil magma-made monster could exist either. Clearly, what I believed and what was real were two entirely different things.

Eddie and Laura still planned to board from the rear while I boarded the front with Scarr, our new objective being to meet in the middle. And, while none of us were too keen on the idea of splitting up, this plan meant that if either party was caught and made unable to continue, the other could potentially set them free or, at the very least, the division itself would force the cultists to divide, making it overall easier to both take on Allister and save Camille.

I had scarcely arrived at my position near the front of the train when a quick scuffling sound echoed quietly from inside the lead car. I listened intently, waiting for someone to sound the alarm, but it never came. Instead, I heard what sounded like a thud from somewhere behind me, far into the dirt and brush of the desert.

Scarr's head popped out from the rear of the front car, and he winked in what was clearly his it's all-clear signal. I climbed up the side of the car, taking his hand just as the train whistle blew, and began to lurch forward.

Admittedly, it was odd taking the hand of a gargoyle. With only three fingers and an opposable thumb, his hand felt smaller in my grasp, though I had no doubt in its ability to crush my own if I were to grip it in a manner that challenged his toughness.

Scarr and I began making our way toward the rear of the train, and for a few minutes, it felt like we had lucked out. Most of the cars we encountered were either empty or occupied by no more than one or two cultists, which turned out to be quite an easy undertaking for a detective with a gargoyle sidekick.

When we arrived at the sixth or seventh car, however, we came to a dead stop. "How the hell are we supposed to get by that?" I asked, looking at my silent companion. He shrugged, then tilted his head and shifted his stare to the distance as if he were considering the situation.

The car was packed to the brim with cultists. There were perhaps thirty or so of them spread throughout the oddly lavish passenger car, and while most of them appeared to either be comfortably settled in or already fast asleep, there were still several cultists who were awake and alert, and quite possibly, ready for our eventual appearance.

Going through the car might have been possible if I had a disguise and weren't carrying a magical sword of ice wrapped in cloth over my shoulder. But since only one of these things would be possible to achieve, it appeared I had no other choice than to cross the train from atop the car.

Obviously, Scarr could simply take to the sky and land on the other side, but that wasn't an option for me. "I guess we don't have much of a choice," I said as I made my way over to the steel pegs that acted as a ladder to the top of the car. "Up and over it is."

I hoisted myself up and began making my way across the roof of the car. I was just beginning to think about how cool it was to be walking across the top of a moving train when, about one-third of the way across, a large brute of a man appeared, blocking my way to the other side. His robe scarcely fit him, and while I wanted to imagine that this guy was no more than a large teddy bear, the grizzly scar that he wore across his face told of a different kind of man.

"Easy now, big fella," I said, reaching for my Colt. "I'd rather not kill you, but I will if I have to."

I didn't really have a problem with shooting the guy if he got in my way, but the noise from my revolver would definitely alert the cultists in the car below, and the chaos that would certainly follow would make it a lot more challenging to take Allister by surprise.

My threats went unheeded, and just as I thought I was going to have to pull the trigger, Scarr appeared behind the hulking threat, and in one swift motion, took hold of the tower's tightly fitted robes and thrust him effortlessly off the side of the moving train.

I watched as the massive figure soared through the air. It was dark, and while it was impossible to see the look on his face, I was certain his smug expression had disappeared only to be replaced by that of pure terror as he plummeted a good eighty feet to the ground. Scarr clapped his hands together and smiled.

"I'm glad you're on our side," I yelled just loud enough to be heard over the sound of the wind as the train continued its steady pace through the mountainous terrain of the Andes.

After descending the ladder, I peered through the window on the rear side of the train car to see that none of its occupants had become aware of our presence. "I suppose he was just a roaming guard; we're going to need to be careful," I said, looking to Scarr, who nodded in agreement. We turned and once again began making our way through the cars headed toward the rear of the train.

Laura panted as she regained her footing. She had nearly toppled backward when she missed the rail of the caboose by a mere inch. Thankfully, Eddie had jumped aboard the train first and turned to do the only thing natural to a gentleman, offering her his hand, which turned into more of a swooping gesture than anything else.

"That was close," Eddie said, pointing out the obvious. Laura let go of his hand and straightened her shirt.

"Let us hope that's it for mishaps," she replied, drawing her PPK. Eddie followed suit and drew his own P.38 before risking a glance through the rear window of the caboose. "You Know, Eddie," Laura said, "maybe you were too harsh on that poor kid."

She was, of course, referencing the cultist who had taken Eddie's gun. "Kid got precisely what he deserved. Besides, a few of the cultists remained behind; someone's bound to find him sooner or later and give him back his silly robe."

Just prior to getting into position to board the train, Eddie had taken the cultist by surprise and tied him to the framework of an unfinished building using his own sash, leaving him bare of all articles of his clothing.

"Looks empty," he said, returning his focus to the train car. "I'll head in first, and you follow." Laura thought about the idea for a moment before holstering her gun.

"Not that your idea is a bad idea," she said honestly, "but what do you say we try something a little different? I'll go in first, and you keep an eye on me. If someone happens to be inside, wait until it looks like they're buying my 'I'm lost' ruse, and then you take 'em from behind."

Eddie nodded in agreement, smiling at the idea of Laura playing the damsel in distress. Laura raised an eyebrow at him then entered the train, closing the door behind her.

Eddie watched as she made her way to the end of the train uninterrupted. He was about to enter when a man stepped out from a little doorway right next to the door that Laura had entered. He ducked for a moment until he was positive the man hadn't seen him, then looked back inside to see the man approaching Laura. "You shouldn't be here." Eddie heard him say.

"Oh, I'm sorry," Laura replied. "I was looking for the bathroom, and you know how confusing these trains can be."

The man's face remained dour, and it was clear that he wasn't buying her story. He stared at her for a moment before reaching for what appeared to be an intercom just as Eddie opened the door gun trained. "I wouldn't do that if I were you."

"Your timing could not have been better," Laura said, drawing her gun and making her way over to the cultist. "Hands up," she said, and she began patting the cultist down. She pulled a small key from his robe and tossed it to Eddie.

"Anything else?" Eddie said, catching the key with his free hand. Laura finished searching him and then pulled free his sash from its position around his waist.

"No, that's it," she said before barking orders at the cultists to put his hands behind his back.

This wasn't the first time Eddie and Laura had worked together. She had become an intricate part of the Ray Shields Detective Agency, and she didn't always just answer the phones and sit behind a desk. In fact, Laura and Eddie had worked together on numerous occasions where it was her and not Eddie who had been responsible for the successful outcome of the case.

When she finished tying the cultist's hands behind his back, she forced him into a seat at the rear of the caboose and stuffed a torn piece of his robe in his mouth.

"Don't worry, I'm sure someone will find you eventually, dear," she said with a whisper, her posture somewhat reassuring. Then, with the same coolness that she had worn the entire interaction, she gave him one quick swat to the forehead with the butt of her pistol.

"You always have a way of making that look good." Eddie nudged the guy with his foot. Convinced that the coldcocked cultist wasn't getting up, he walked over to the door and peered through. Unlike the caboose, the cars ahead didn't have windows on the doors, making it impossible to know what was on the other side.

Earlier, they had also noted that a handful of the boxcars didn't have front and rear doors, meaning they would have to traverse the car from above and search it through a hatch at the top.

Scarr had been sure to make clear which cars would have to be crossed in this way, and while it did make sense that he be the one to check them out, the train would not be moving too quickly through the mountainous terrain, so Eddie insisted that Scarr help Ray at the front instead.

Eddie opened the door to the caboose and stepped through. The sound of the train's wheels on the track echoed through the night, and it became clear to him that every time they opened one of these doors, the occupants of the next car would immediately become aware of their presence.

Laura closed the door behind her and looked at Eddie. "I guess we're gonna have to do this the hard way," she said.

Eddie rolled the key around in his hand for a moment, then placed it in the lock on the door. He gave a slight nod of his head as it turned and replied, "At least we don't have to shoot our way in." The lock clicked, and they pushed the door open, guns drawn.

They kept their guns at the ready as they moved toward the front of the car, but instead of encountering more cultists, they found themselves surrounded by a large number of wooden crates and nothing more. Laura gawked at the sheer number of crates crammed into this single car as she holstered her weapon and began searching for a way to open them.

"Eddie, can you—"

She was about to ask him if he could help when he replied, "Already ahead of you." Eddie walked to the end of the car and grabbed a crowbar that was propped against the far wall. She smiled at him, then seeing a crate labeled 'this way up,' with the arrow facing the wall, she knocked the tall container over onto its side.

Eddie cringed at the dull thud of the crate hitting the floor and looked over his shoulder at the door. He half expected it to fling open, letting in a dozen cultists, thus ending their mission before it ever really began. With his head still craned toward the door, he decided that the sound was most likely masked by the train's constant swaying on the tracks, and he turned back to Laura. "Could you keep it down a little?"

She smiled and looked at him. "What's the matter, Eddie, afraid of a little action?"

He scoffed at the comment and then finished making his way over toward Laura and the crate.

It hadn't taken him but three solid pries with the crowbar to open the crate, and once the lid was carefully placed on the ground per his request, Laura hesitantly began pulling out the protective straw that lined the box. Eddie was the first of them to back away from the crate, followed by Laura's look of disgust and the dropping of the large clay arm that she pulled out.

"The hell?" Eddie said as he bent down to pick up the appendage. Laura took a moment to recover from her shudders, then grabbed an armful of hay and thrust it aside.

Once the crate's contents were fully visible, it became clear why this particular crate was so large. Inside, laying separated like the skeletal remains of a body on the examination table, was the clay shell of a young, and oddly enough, very lifelike-looking woman.

She was, or rather would be if she were pieced together, a tall, athletic type with long-toned arms and arguably longer and even more well-shaped legs that were most certainly very carefully crafted. Her face was youthful and gentle and carried with it the same realism. Yet, like the rest of her, it was still and lifeless. In all, save for the oddly shaped hole in the center of her chest and the arm that lay in pieces behind Eddie, the clay figure was flawless.

"Any other day, I'd say that we just found the work of Michelangelo's prodigy," Eddie said, taking in the detail of the clay woman. "But my gut's telling me there is something far more sinister going on here than just art class."

Laura chuckled at the comment. "I don't even want to know what you find sinister about art class Eddie," she said. Eddie shrugged his shoulders and picked the crowbar up from off the lid. He turned on his heels, walked over to the nearest medium-sized crate, and began to open it.

Closer examination of the crates revealed several more larger crates tucked under or behind smaller ones. Upon opening them, it was clear that these crates were indeed not intended for a classroom filled with wide-eyed art students. Instead, the contents of the crates ranged from assorted clay limbs, of which none looked to be anything less than perfect representations of the human form, to vials filled with a reddish, mercury-like substance.

Eddie held one of the vials in his hands and ran his thumb along its glass surface, studying the reaction that the red liquid inside was having to the presence of life. He looked at Laura. "I know our primary objective here is to find Camii—" he paused, letting out a long sigh of frustration. "But whatever use Allister has planned for these, we can't be the ones that let it happen."

Laura nodded her head in agreement, then raised her arm and playfully pushed a smaller open crate filled with vials to the floor.

* * *

Scarr and I had managed to make it several more cars toward the rear of the train before having to make our way across the roof of another cultist-filled car. Up until this point, the cars were void of any cultists, but we did manage to find a few maps that appeared to be of importance, so I quickly relieved Allister and his underlings of them.

Naturally, having made it so far with such little resistance, I wasn't worried that we were being followed, but I did realize that if we were discovered, finding a way to slow down the cultists in these cars would be imperative to our ability to escape.

This is where Scarr's gargoyle strength came in handy. Borrowing some steel from the railing, Scarr managed to bar the doors on both sides of the car shut by jamming a few pieces of railing straight through the deck in front of the doors. Quite literally raising the bar of his worth as the newest member of the Ray Shields Detective Agency.

The next car was entirely empty, save for a few buckets and shovels lying in the far corner. I was about to open the door leading out when Scarr stopped me. That's when I heard the voices. Between the noise of the train and the fact that there was a door between me and whoever was on the other side of this door, the voices were simply muffled.

I stepped next to the door, gun at the ready, and placed my ear firm against the wall. I was hoping to eavesdrop on the party outside, but my decision to do so was too late. The low thud of a door closing, followed by silence, was all that was to be heard.

Scarr and I exchanged glances, and just as I was about to open the door for a second time, the loud, unmistakable sound of gunfire erupted from the next car. I dropped to the floor just as a bullet splintered the wood of the wall where I had been standing. Collecting myself, I managed to get in a crouching position on the sidewall and was about to return fire when everything went quiet.

I looked to Scarr, who, like myself, had sought to make himself as little a target as possible by crouching close to the other sidewall. For a moment, he appeared to be poised to strike, waiting in ambush for anyone who came through the door. Then his rigid posture relaxed, and he stood up and looked at me, and with the familiar motioning of his tail, he beckoned me to follow.

I rose from my position against the wall and made my way over toward the door. "Are you sure it's safe?" I asked. My own senses now on high alert. He gave a nod, smiled, and let out another of his unintelligible attempts to vocally communicate; "Scraeddie."

I was on the verge of opening the door for the third time when I realized what he had just said. I looked back at him in complete surprise, and it must have been clear to him by the look of total shock on my face that he had been successful in his attempt to say Eddie's name because he gave perhaps the biggest grin I had seen from him yet.

"Eddie is in the next car?" I said, unnecessarily confirming what I already knew. Scarr nodded, reaching his hand out to pull the door open the rest of the way for me.

He stepped through the door and was already halfway done opening the next door before I was able to free myself of the shocked expression and follow him.

As we entered the room, I saw that Eddie was just standing up from checking the status of the two cultists who he had just exchanged gunfire with, and Laura was in the middle of trying to pry open the door to what appeared to be a jail cell in the middle of the car. Inside that cell was Camille, who, like her sister-in-arms, was attempting to do the same.

"Ray," Eddie said, holstering his weapon. "Boy, am I glad you're here; we could really use some help getting Cami here out of this cage."

He hurriedly grabbed hold of the end of the same long metal bar that Laura was using and began trying to pry the cage bars aside. "Scraahelp."

Eddie and Laura both looked over at Scarr with the same shocked expressions that I just had. Camille also seemed a little surprised by the talking gargoyle, but I ventured to guess that she was more surprised to see him than by the fact that he just spoke.

"You think that's something? You should hear him say your name, Eddie." Eddie looked at Scarr, who returned the comment with another broad smile.

Scarr and I quickly made our way over to the cell, and as I was about to try my hand at helping Laura and Eddie pry the bars open, Scarr stepped up to the cell, placed one hand on each bar, and with tensed muscles, let out a low, strained "Scraaaaacc."

The bars bent in his grasp, leaving a two-foot gap between them. He then stepped back, smiling at us, and bowed playfully.

"Would you look at that," Eddie said as he walked over and gave Scarr a pat on the back. "I'm gonna have to watch out for you," he continued, "or else Ray here might go replacing me with a more obedient and reliable partner."

Scarr proudly smiled at the comment, then turned to Camille, offering her his hand.

Camille hesitantly took it and allowed him to help her through the bars. Once she was out, she turned toward her brother and nearly leaped from Scarr's grasp into the arms of her brother. "Thank heavens you're OK."

The worry in her voice was clear, and it seemed all Eddie could do to hold back his own cry of relief was to hold her tightly. Scarr tilted his head, then seemed to acknowledge the reasoning of this gesture and stepped away to give the siblings space.

Eddie loosed the embrace of his sister and took a step back. "Don't worry, we're getting out of here. Ray," he said, turning his attention to me. "Laura and I have a plan for getting us out of here, and we already managed to possibly slow Allister down with one of his ventures. Tell me you've got the amulet and kicked that—"

Eddie trailed off, looking at his sister, then looked back to me. "No, we never saw him," I said, "but we have Camille now, and I'm pretty sure these maps will tell us where he's going."

I held the rolled-up maps out in front of me and was about to suggest we take a quick look at them when we heard a commotion back from the direction Scarr and I had come from.

"Looks like we got company," I said instead. "Eddie, you said you guys have a plan for getting us off this train."

"Right," Eddie responded, then grabbed his sister's hand and began making his way to the door at the rear of the car. "This way."

Laura, Scarr, and I followed suit and trailed them through the next three cars, passing three very unhappily tied up and gagged cultists along the way. When we made our way into the fourth car, Eddie stopped and turned back to face me. "End of the line, boss," he said, glancing through the door behind me.

"What do you mean end of the line?" I said, unsure as to why we were stopping somewhere in the middle of the train.

"I mean, it's the end of the line, boss," he said again before Laura chimed in.

"Eddie and I found some unsettling things in those crates they were loading onto the train earlier, so we decided to relieve Allister of them."

"Ahhh," I said, realizing what they had done.

"The Dynamic Dou strikes again," Eddie joshed, raising his left hand and then tossing it away from his head, two fingers raised to the eyebrow in a mock salute. "Sometimes I forget how effective a team you two can be."

"So, what now?" Camille asked hastily, her voice betraying her concern about the pose trying to make its way in our direction. "Now," Eddie boomed, confidently sticking out his chest. "Now, we put a little distance between that mob and us. Laura," Eddie said, turning toward her.

"Way ahead of you."

Laura and Eddie made their way back through the door at the front of the car, where Laura then lay flat on her belly, and Eddie grabbed hold of the waist of her pants with one hand and the rail with the other.

As I watched Laura and Eddie working in tandem, I couldn't help but recall the first time the pair took on a case together. I was out of the office sick with the flu, and, per Laura's persistent demands, I let her and Eddie handle the Gofman account. Mrs. Gofman had come to me, certain that her husband was gambling away all their money.

The trouble of it all was that Mr. Gofman worked in one of the most secure buildings in the city. A factor that had thus far kept Eddie and me from gaining access. And up until then, none of our tailing efforts turned anything up that would suggest Mr. Gofman as being anything but a stand-up husband.

Putting Laura on the case turned out to be the best thing that could happen. Turns out one of the security guards on duty that day was a Frenchman, and Laura, with all her charms and possibly her legs, was able to seduce him into paying just enough attention to her that she was able to swipe his access card, giving her and Eddie a means to entering the building.

The two of them managed to use the side entrance and take the stairs up to the fourteenth floor, arriving just in time to catch Mr. Gofman red-handed and in an illegal online match of seven-card stud. Needless to say, Eddie's threats proved quite an effective deterrent for Mr. Gofman's gambling addiction, and his wife was very pleased to have both the attention of her husband and his money safely back home.

I laughed, and for a moment, the idea of Eddie and Laura handling our escape alleviated any nervousness about our getting away safely. An alleviation that faded just as quickly as it arose. I looked up to see Eddie and Laura come hurdling through the door, landing hard on the floor in front of me.

I drew my Colt and took aim as the slender figure of the man that I had seen a day before, standing behind Eddie in the projection room of the old theater, stepped into the car, followed closely by Allister. This time, I didn't hesitate. I shifted my aim and fired two well-placed rounds at the cult leader's chest.

The man in front of him moved with unbelievable speed, stepping directly in the path of the bullets in the blink of an eye. Both shots struck him center mass within an inch of each other, and yet he didn't even flinch. Hell, he didn't even bleed. The man grinned, then, as quickly as he had moved to stop the bullets, he leaned forward and, before I could even think to move, charged, striking me with the fastest right hook imaginable.

I dropped to one knee from the blow and tried to recover by bringing my gun to point in the direction he had just been; I was too slow. Another blow came from my left, knocking me hard against the wall and my gun out of my hand. The sound of several shots echoed from the far side of the car, and I recognized the sound of Laura's Walther PPK.

I looked up to see the slender man shift his stance, ready to charge her. Laura was a crack shot, so I know she hit him, yet he still seemed unphased. I tried to reach for his foot but was too slow, and as I braced for the worst, I saw Scarr imitate the man's initial actions, stepping between Laura and the speeding man's path.

Scarr had raised his arms in a crossed fashion and absorbed the full force of the man's blow without even moving. The menacing grin on the man's face disappeared, only to be replaced with a look of anger and frustration. Scarr returned the gesture, digging the claws of his right foot into the deck of the car before thrusting the man, and himself, straight up and through the roof.

Wood splintered around us, and as much as I wanted to watch Scarr skillfully toy with the man in an aerial battle, I could sense that the odds were still tilted against us. I turned my attention back toward Allister, only to see that he was already holding the amulet in front of him. I looked around quickly for my pistol, but it was nowhere to be found.

That's when I remembered the sword. I reached back to grab the sword by the hilt, only to feel that it was no longer there. It must have torn free when I was knocked across the car.

Flustered, I grabbed the first piece of debris I could and thrust it. The amulet was beginning to glow red just as the sharpened end of the splintered wood hit Allister square in the shoulder. He dropped the charged amulet, grabbed the pseudo stake, and pulled it free from his shoulder with a silent but painful and angry look on his face.

I rose to charge him only to be gifted with a sharp pain in my right side. Apparently, the second blow from the unknown man, if he were even a man, had done more damage than I had realized, and I was quickly brought back to one knee. "Eddie!"

"On it, boss," he bellowed as he lunged forward toward Allister.

I watched, ready to see Allister take the full force of Eddie's shoulder when the ceiling exploded for a second time sending sharp wooden bits of shrapnel in all directions. Eddie was nearly hit by the body that came barreling through the ceiling, forcing him to abandon his charge and leap out of the way.

"Oh, my." I heard Laura gasp from over my shoulder, and as I recovered from my defensive position, I looked up to see that Eddie was kneeling over the crumpled body of our gargoyle companion. He was still and unresponsive to Eddie's attempts at getting him to come to. Camille was rushing past me toward her brother when Laura appeared at my side, her pistol aimed directly at Allister.

The sound of her gun going off next to me was almost a relief. I was certain that this time Allister was finished. But as quickly as the comfort had come, it was gone. Allister was standing there with the amulet raised, a look of pure evil in his eyes.

Everything seemed to move in slow motion; the amulet roared to life, releasing an almost invisible wave that can only be described as resembling something like the heat waves that you see on the road on a hot summer's day. The concussion rippled across the car, first hitting Eddie and Scarr, then Camille, before reaching Laura and me, and we were all thrust up, nearly to the ceiling, before being slammed hard against the ground.

I gasped, trying to catch my breath. I could barely move from the pain alone, but I managed to roll over and start to rise when I felt the hold of that invisible force; Allister was once again in control. It was all I could do to look around with my eyes and see that my friends were all similarly incapacitated.

Laura was behind me a few feet, pinned against the wall, and Scarr lay as he had been right next to Eddie, whose anger was definitely beyond that of anything I had seen in him before. That's when I realized Camille was not next to her brother.

I struggled to tilt my head, managing to do so just enough to see Allister standing face-to-face with Camille, her body suspended in front of him. The slender man was back at his side and judging from the grimace on his face, I could tell his fight with Scarr had taken a lot from him.

"I've underestimated your friends," Allister said, running his finger down her cheek. "Perhaps I should have killed them when I had the chance. Well, better late than never," he said, turning toward us.

"Skogh lach Ta!" Camille blurted out. And the hold on her was released. When she dropped to the floor, I thought that I could feel the same invisible force holding me back weaken, but when I tried to move, I found that I was still under the influence of the amulet and all I could do was watch.

Camille quickly pulled free a knife from her boot and thrust it up toward Allister. She was fast, but the slender man, even in his weakened state, was faster.

He moved between Allister and Camille, catching her by the wrist. "There, there," Allister said, making his way out from behind his loyal defender, his grating voice piercing the silence of the now still car. "You're beginning to be more trouble than you're worth."

"Screw you," Camille said, gritting her teeth as she struggled to free herself from the slender man's grasp. "You'll never get away with this Bennings, You piece of—"

Allister slapped her hard, and she hung her head, tears beginning to stream down her cheeks.

"Stop it! Let her go!" Eddie yelled. It was clear Eddie was doing everything he could to fight the invisible force holding him down. I even thought for a moment that he was on the verge of breaking free, but his binding held firm and Eddie was as helpless as the rest of us.

Allister looked at Eddie, then grabbed Camille by the hair and thrust her head back. "You think you're clever, don't you, girl."

Camille spit, and he jerked back wiping, the foreign mix of saliva, snot, and tears, from his face. He stared at her for a moment, then shook his head. "You know, I think we can get along with only a part of you after all."

He looked at the slender man, giving him a slight nod. The man pulled back his free hand, holding it there as if waiting for something, then, his eyes turned black, and his fingers grew several inches in length until they were razor-sharp points.

"NO!" Eddie screamed as the slender man thrust his hand deep into Camille's chest. "STOP! Please!" Eddie's yells were desperate, and I could feel his own heart being ripped away just as the man pulled free from Camille, her own still-beating heart.

"Aaaaaaaaaaaahhhhhhhhhhhh!" Eddie's screams were of pure hatred, anger, and terror and my own heart broke as I watched my partner die inside. "I am going to kill you, you bastard!" he screamed with all the power his voice could muster. "I am going to kill you!"

The slender man tossed Camille's lifeless body next to Eddie and turned to face his master. "Perfect, my child. Let us go. Perhaps this will have broken their spirits."

Allister and the slender man turned and walked through the now open doorway, crossing over to the next car. "Trying to stop me will only lead to more suffering, Ray," Allister hollered back before looking at Camille's lifeless body. "Pity," he said.

Allister then nodded to the man holding Camille's heart. With his other hand, he cut free the car from the rest of the train, and together they turned and entered the departing train.

Chapter 15

"Useless! Stupid! Why? Why?" My partner's cries drowned out any noise from outside the slowing train car, and without mercy, every convulsing sob and shout of anger was felt in full effect by the rest of us. His large hands were wrapped around her shoulders as he desperately tried to rouse her. He shook her, demanding that she return to life.

"Oh, Eddie." Laura's tone was soft and heartfelt. She approached him with subtle hesitation and kneeled beside him, placing her still shaking hand on his. "Eddie, I'm so sorry, sweetie," she said, tears welling in her own eyes. Eddie ignored her attempt to console him and buried his face deep into the side of his sister's neck.

The hate that I felt for Allister was pure, and while it could never rival Eddie's, there was no doubt that Allister would not be the one walking away the next time we met. He had taken everything from my closest friend, leaving him a torn man, once again broken and destined to be nothing more than a fragment of who he once was, and there was absolutely nothing that I could do to prevent that.

"Scraeddieee." Scarr was standing, albeit awkwardly propped up against the wall with his tail, and his words, if one would call them that, were faint. "Scraeddie," his voice echoed, though barely louder than a murmur.

Eddie pulled his head free from its burrow and looked in the direction of Scarr. Scarr's lip furrowed like the brow of a saddened child before losing all expression, and he collapsed to the floor.

I was closer to him than Eddie, and yet it was Eddie who reached Scarr's crumpled figure first. When Scarr collapsed, Eddie's reaction was instant. Tears still streaming down his face, he lunged forward, nearly tripping in his haste to reach his falling friend. It was as if in that very instant Eddie was confronted with the fear of losing another ward and, in recognizing the urgency to tend to Scar's wounds, he abandoned his sister's still body purely out of the need to protect Scarr from suffering the same fate.

Laura and I watched as Eddie took Scarr into his arms and pulled his flask free from its home inside his jacket. He fumbled with the cap until it nearly ripped off from the force of his haste and then lifted Scarr's head and tilted the flask.

Considering that I've never known Eddie to carry anything other than Jack in that tin, I could only assume that the clear liquid that poured from the flask was nothing other than water. "Come on then," Eddie said as he struggled to get our gargoyle friend to swallow.

After a few more attempts, Scarr finally managed to down some of the water and regain consciousness. "That a boy," Eddie said, smiling in relief. "Let's get you fixed up."

Eddie's full attention was on Scarr for the time being, and he was in the middle of bandaging Scarr's wounds with scraps of his own jacket when I noticed Laura, who was still kneeling beside Camille. She had taken advantage of

Eddie's distraction and covered Camille's body with some kind of painter's tarp that had been lying in the corner. I locked eyes with her for a moment before quickly looking away.

Nothing could compare to the pain Eddie was in right now, but the shame that I felt for letting his sister die after she had put so much faith in me to stop Allister was most definitely high. If only I had managed to hold on to the sword, maybe I could have harnessed all that power that I felt when I pulled it free, maybe I would have been able to stop Allister before he could use the amulet, maybe—

"Ray." I felt Laura place her hand on my shoulder as she began to speak to me. "Ray, this isn't your fault. And it's not Eddie's or Scarr's or mine," she said, raising her voice loud enough to be heard by Eddie and Scarr as well. "This is Allister's fault. He is the one responsible for Camille's death," she paused a moment to stifle an upwelling of emotion, and in doing so, she radiated with that same confident calm as before in the cave.

"Camille died fighting to the very end. She put everything she had into trying to stop Allister, and we owe it to her to do the same." Eddie glanced at his sister's covered body, then went back to tending Scar's wounds. "We can't stop now. We just can't. Ray, you said you had an idea where he was going, right." I nodded my head and began to look around for the maps. "Then we need to do everything we can to get there and stop Allister."

"She's right," Eddie said, wiping away the tears that threatened another downpour. "Camille wouldn't have it any other way."

Eddie was certainly among the best at suppressing his emotions, but as I looked at him, his eyes locking with mine, I realized that he wasn't hiding them. He was drawing strength from the anger and the pain, and it was sure to be his driving force for revenge. "We have to find Allister and put a stop to this."

Eddie's voice was now a force of sheer determination, and it was a relief to hear. I knew my partner was never going to be the same again, but if just the hope of avenging his sister gave him this much life, then perhaps the actual thing would give him a fighting chance at normalcy.

"You're right," I said. Moving to retrieve the maps from under a pile of broken wood in the corner of the car. When I grabbed them, I noticed the tail end of the cloth I had used to wrap the sword. Instantly, the motivation that Eddie and Laura had given me vanished, only to be replaced again with anger.

I yanked the sword free from under the debris, knotted the rope that made for a sling, and thrust it over my shoulder. "Eddie," I said, anger welling in my voice. "We're going to end this all right. We're going to make that son of a bitch pay for what he did, and we're not going to stop until every syllable of Monstre de Ténèbres is washed from the tongues of those who call themselves believers."

Eddie glanced at his sister's now covered body and stared. He seemed to consider my words, then turned his attention back to Scarr, helping him to his feet before hoisting him onto his back. "That's what she would want," he said, then turned, one arm across his chest, holding onto Scarr's hand, the other reaching for the door.

"Eddie, wait," Laura called out to him.

"There's no time for that," he replied before she could even make the suggestion, then opened the door and stepped through.

Laura and I looked at one another, and while we both knew that burying Camille would perhaps leave Eddie with a little more comfort at the end of all this, we also recognized the same urgency to find Allister before it was too late.

Laura took one step toward the door, stopped, turned on her heel, and walked back to Camille's body. She kneeled beside it, pulled the blanket free from its covering, and whispered something into her ear. She then picked up the knife that Camille had tried to use to kill Allister and looked it over.

The blade was dark, nearly black, with a single symbol etched into the side of it. I couldn't make out what it was from where I was, but I'm certain neither of us could read it. Laura gripped the dark brown handle, then reached for Camille's boot and took the sheath.

"Let's go, Ray," she said as she stood and made her way toward the door.

"Go on," I said. "I'll catch up." She nodded and followed after Eddie.

I stood there alone, surrounded by feelings of failure and hate and confusion. This was the worst day that the Ray Shields Detective Agency had ever had, and at that very moment, I could not see how we would ever recover from the loss. One of our own had been taken from us, and while I knew that we all felt the burden of responsibility for Camille's death, it was my job to keep my team safe, and I failed.

My anger, while in large directed at Allister, was also in part inward. I looked at Camille and grit my teeth. "Camille," I said quietly. "You were everything to Eddie, all that man ever had, even when he didn't really have you at all. Do me a favor and look after him, from wherever you are, and I promise you, here and now, that I will always do my best to make sure he doesn't forget who he is, who you helped him to become."

I bowed my head and let the tears that hung in my eyes fall quietly to the floor.

I turned, lifted my head, and followed my friends out the door.

Chapter 16

Eddie's gaze over the deserted horizon was interrupted when he saw what he thought was the silhouette of Ray and Laura crest the hills to the south. The pair had been gone for half the night, and he was beginning to wonder if they had found the town indicated on the map from the train or if they had succumbed to the heat and harshties of the desert. It wasn't them.

He dipped the blood-soaked cloth into the kettle, taking care not to burn himself, and rang it only after the rag had cooled enough to do so.

Scarr was in bad shape, and he needed every ounce of help that Eddie could offer him. The gargoyle had risked its life to protect Eddie and his friends, and despite having lost his sister to the very being Scarr had failed to defeat, he would not give in; he would not let Scarr become another of that vile thing's victims.

"Scraa—Aaac," Scarr managed to let out a low and broken cry as Eddie pressed the rag against the wound at his side. He was in better shape than he had been, but even, holding true to legend, with his ability to recuperate during the day while turned entirely to stone, his injuries were extensive, and Eddie constantly had to change the dressings on the two wounds that were so deep that they simply refused to close. Even as a statue, the gargoyle bled.

"Settle down," he said, stilling the gargoyle. "Just lay back and rest."

Eddie directed his gaze toward the rising sun and scanned the horizon again. Something else that Eddie had learned was that gargoyles don't always turn to stone during the day. From what he was able to learn by taking care of Scarr, it was a preference more than anything. Whatever the case, Scarr was being difficult and was refusing to turn this morning.

Eddie shook his head, and his thoughts drifted back to worrying about his partner's whereabouts. Part of him desperately wanted Ray and Laura to return. Being alone with his thoughts was the last thing he needed right now, and yet he couldn't help but feel some level of relief knowing that the two of them were nowhere to be found.

He was angrier than he could ever remember being, and he feared that his ability to control that anger wouldn't last if they continued to check up on him.

He sat back, looking again to Scarr, then he stoked the fire with what was left of the long stick that he had been using for the past two days, then bowed his head. He knew they meant well, he really did, but he also knew that Ray felt responsible, and that was enough to make him even angrier. Sure, Ray had good reason to feel the way he did, but it wasn't him that ran Camille through and ripped out her heart.

Eddie tightened his grip on the stick as he pulled it from the fire and watched it burn. The flames that danced on the end of it were wild, and for a moment, he smiled, remembering how free and wild his sister had once been. In her youth, she was always looking for adventure, constantly sharing ideas on where they could go when they finally had the means to do so. He regretted never having had the opportunity to make any of those adventures a reality.

The thought quickly faded, and for what seemed like the thousandth time, all that he could think about was her eyes in those final moments when her life left them. Eddie stood, throwing the stick as far as he could, and shouted at the top of his lungs before crumpling to the floor, burying his face in his hands. He missed her. He missed her now more than ever before, and he knew it was because now he knew that she was never going to come back.

For so many years, all he had ever hoped for was for his sister to be OK and that she would one day return to him. He had held out, often telling himself that she had suffered some kind of trauma and though she had gotten better, that she suffered from amnesia and just couldn't remember who she was.

He had been content with this idea because he simply wanted for her to be OK. He wanted for her to be off somewhere living a happy life, and in some way, perhaps he was OK with this because this also carried with it the still real possibility that she might one day wake up and remember who she was; that she would remember him.

Eddie's sobs stained his cheeks as he began to understand that none of what he thought had been the case. Sure, his sister had been alive all these years, but she wasn't living.

She had spent what was supposed to be the best years of her life as a prisoner simply trying to survive to the next day, and when she was finally free, she was so wrapped up in the world that had been forced upon her that it was all she knew. She wasn't able to just return home to him. She couldn't just go back to living a normal life and forget about everything that had been forced on her. Allister had taken everything from her, just as he had taken her away from Eddie, and he did it not once but twice.

"Scraaac," Eddie looked up to see Scarr now sitting propped up against the rock that Eddie had been sitting on. "Scraeddieee." The gargoyle smiled at Eddie and removed the bandage at his side to reveal two freshly closed wounds. Eddie stared for a moment, then wiped his tears away, clamoring to his feet in his effort to recompose himself. He laughed while still crying, only this time the tears were a mix of sad ones and happy ones.

"Scraa—scrorry." Scarr's attempt to apologize to Eddie fueled the pour of emotions, and he rushed to the injured gargoyle's side.

"No, no," Eddie said, putting his arm under Scarr's wing to support him as he tried sitting up straight. "You did more than anyone else could have done," he said, using his free hand to wipe the last of the tears from his face. He had lost his sister, and for that, he was devastated, but he had also nearly lost his friend, and he needed to remember who was really responsible.

"We're gonna catch up to 'em, and we're gonna make sure we finish what we started," Eddie paused, then looked sternly over at Scarr. "We're going to finish what Cammie started."

"Scraaac!" Scarr's response was deeper, and while Eddie wasn't sure, it also seemed to carry more purpose, more substance than usual, almost as if he were making Eddie a promise to help him no matter the cost. "Scuurrraa," the gargoyle groaned as he slowly rose to his feet, clearly using Eddie to do so since he was there. Then Scarr stretched out his wings and gave Eddie a nudge.

"You sure you're ready?" Eddie said, clearly concerned with his friend's recovery.

Scarr grinned and turned his head to the sky. He took a little longer than usual, but after a brief moment of what Eddie perceived as mental preparation, Scarr dug his claws into the cracked desert soil beneath his feet, bent his knees, though ever slightly, and leaped with the force of a freight train high into the sky. The burst of air that followed was enough to send the embers of the fire in a frenzy that whirled around Eddie.

Eddie's reaction to the dancing embers that now fell around him was minimal. His focus was on Scarr, but he wasn't watching to see if his friend was all right, the gargoyle may share a certain level of stubbornness with Eddie, but he certainly knew his own limitation.

No, Eddie was thinking about the fight that lay ahead, and he knew that Scarr was too. He watched as the gargoyle spiraled through the air, diving oddly but with purpose, and he sensed that Scarr was rehearsing his flight patterns, likely in response to what he learned fighting that thing that nearly killed him and succeeded in doing so to his friends' sister.

Eddie looked again to the horizon, only to see a still empty skyline. He wanted to wait for Ray and Laura to return, but every second they delayed, Allister and the rest of his cult only got further away and closer to their end game. He knew that they stood a better chance together, but he also understood the importance of time, and he also knew his partner would know how to follow him if he left now.

The embers from the fire once again leaped from their nearly settled places, and Eddie looked over to see Scarr hovering to his right. His wings worked back and forth in long forceful arching motions, similar to the flap of a bird but with a more fanlike stroke toward the bottom, and there was definitely more thrust.

"I guess this means we're on the same page then," Eddie said, locking eyes with Scarr. Scarr simply nodded in response as he effortlessly maintained his position a few feet above the ground, save for his tail which swung carelessly from side to side. "Right then, I'll pack up here, and we can head out. What do you say to a little beef jerky for breakfast?"

Eddie watched as Scarr cocked his head to the side in his usual fashion, indicating his curiosity at learning a new word. "Oh, you're definitely in for a treat." Eddie let out a low chuckle and then started digging into a knapsack.

* * *

The cool desert breeze was a relief against my dry skin, and I was glad that this particular evening in the Atacama was at its end. Laura and I would be back at camp soon, and while I wanted to think that Eddie would have Scarr back on his feet, I wasn't holding my breath. His injuries were so extensive, it was a miracle he even survived.

"I hope Eddie has grieved at least a little in our absence," Laura said, handing me the canteen that she filled in the small trading community we had spent most of the night looking for.

"Me too," I said, giving her an almost routine reply.

She hadn't been on board with us going off in search of a town that we weren't even sure was there while Eddie was left to tend to Scarr, but ultimately what other choice did she have? "It's not OK for him to hold it in like that," she said with a slightly raised tone that betrayed her thus far well-maintained level of annoyance with my partner. "And who does he think he's fooling, anyway?"

Laura's frustration, while almost never visible, was beginning to surface, and since I had never seen her so flustered, I couldn't be sure how her tirade was going to end. At least she was getting it out here, with me, and not back at camp, where she would most certainly be giving Eddie a piece of her mind.

Laura continued to sourly berate my partner's macho man demeanor. At the same time, my own thoughts lingered somewhere between dark and hateful desires of revenge, regret for having not been able to stop Allister's underling from killing Camille, and an overwhelming feeling of anxiety about my expected role in this whole saving the world thing.

From what had learned from the maps, Allister was heading to a lesser-known volcano in south-central Chile called Tinguiririca, far beyond our current location in the desert, and since he already had a significant lead on us, he was most likely summoning the Cherufe as we speak. In which case, the super scary evil that everyone has been talking about would be showing its face any moment now, and my anticipation would be over.

"Ray, Ray, are you even listening to me?" I turned in my saddle to see Laura glaring at me with a scornful look in her eyes. "You haven't heard a word I said, have you?" she said, letting out a sigh, then softening her stare. I returned her look of mental exertion with one of my own, and we both looked back to the horizon.

"Camp should be just over this ridge," I said as the horses nudged us ever closer to our companions. But just as we crested the hill and as I was about to apologize to her, I noticed our campfire was burning low, and I couldn't make out any figures beside it. "Damn it," I muttered instead, resulting in a look of confusion from her before she realized my frustration was not directed at her.

Hurrying to dismount as we made it to the camp did nothing more than make air-born the dust that had settled on my saddle during our ride, and as I began to assess the condition of the camp, it was all that seemed out of place. There was no indication that a struggle had taken place, there was no hurriedly packed camp, Eddie and Scarr were just gone, and it was clear that nothing bad had happened here.

I began to worry that Eddie had grown worried for us, tossed Scarr on the back of his horse, and came looking.

"Ray, over here," I turned to see Laura crouched by the fire running her hands through the sand, revealing the cloth-wrapped sword that had been partially buried there. Her other hand was extended in my direction with a small piece of paper in it. I took it and read it out loud. *"Scarr feeling better—Going after Allister—Catch up.*

"Well, Eddie never was one to wait around," I said, tossing the note into the fire. "And it looks like he gave the map a once-over too before he left." I pointed in the direction of our makeshift table atop a small stone slab. "Well, no use in waiting around here, let's get th—" I stopped mid-sentence when I looked back to Laura and saw her standing there with the sword tightly gripped in both hands, its cloth wrapping discarded at her side.

"Laura, are you all right?" I asked. She didn't immediately reply. Instead, her grip on the sword seemed to tighten, and she gave it a long, almost deep, meaningful, once-over. Her head tilted slowly toward the sky with just as much caress, and her eyes never left the blade. Then she brought her head back down, resting her gaze on the hilt.

The blade, still in its upright position, moved closer to her body, and she began to slowly wave it around as if she were testing its weight. "It has been a very long time," she said.

When she spoke, there was a certain quality in her voice that was almost ethereal, and while she still sounded like Laura, this was the second time I had seen her in a trance-like state while in such close proximity to the sword. "Who are you?" I asked hesitantly, my posture becoming noticeably uncomfortable.

"Don't worry, Ray," she replied, her eyes briefly ceasing their assault on the sword. "My adorable little sister is still with us." She smiled, and her eyes returned to their fixed gaze on the sword.

"Sister," I spoke under my breath and tilted my head toward the ground, much like I do when I find myself thinking too hard about any puzzling part of a case. What did she mean by that?

"Come on, Ray," she said, taking a few steps back, the swaying of the sword becoming more pronounced the further away she got. "Oh, come now, it's really not that hard to figure out, what with all the obscenely crazy things you've seen over the past few weeks."

The sword was almost dancing in her hands now, and the way she moved was so natural. It was as if she had carried this sword her entire life. "Wha—" I stopped before the question even finished forming in my mouth and looked back down.

"Magic swords of ice, warrior daughters." My head shot up in recognition of what she was insinuating.

"How is that even possible? That would make her hundreds if not thousands of years old."

She smirked at the comment. "Oh, much older than that, Ray. Don't disappoint me, Ray. Is it that hard for you to believe that your dear Laura is actually a goddess reincarnate?"

She seemed to put emphasis on the former half of the word and subtly let the latter role from her tongue. "Think about it, Ray, just think. She came to you haunted by a presence you never found; she mysteriously misses work the day you first encountered the cult; that haunting presence has returned and grows stronger the closer you get to the Cherufe's location."

She stopped her choreograph-like movements with the sword, then looked at me with a more serious gaze.

"She is still your Laura, Ray, but she is also still my sister. She is a daughter of Antu, brightest of all Pillan, keeper of light, and the Cherufe senses her presence. He can feel the power of the amulet that this Allister character has, and he is simply waiting to be set free so that he can come for her. If that happens, Ray, you will be the only chance she has at defeating him, just as she will be the only chance you have."

"And what does that even mean beyond our destinies being intertwined?" I was beginning to dislike all the allusion toward my being the best hope for humanity with a side of absolutely zero clue as to how I was supposed to achieve saving the world.

"So far, all you or anyone else has managed to say is that really bad things are coming, and I have to stop it, but you haven't said a thing about how I am supposed to do that." My irritation must have been apparent because Laura, or rather her sister if that was in fact what was possessing her, raised her eyebrow at me in disapproval.

"Ray," she said, this time with more clarity in her voice, "It is not the way of the Pillan to question the Kueyen, for it is self-balancing and ever-present."

I shook my head, somewhat disapproving of her answer, and replied questioningly. "Kueyen," I said, with a puzzled look on my face.

"It is what you call—the universe." She smiled and let the sword rest at her side before approaching and placing her hand on my cheek.

"Our existence," she paused, running the tips of her fingers under my chin while her eyes penetrated the depths of my own. "Yours and mine," she continued, "are the same. We are the energies, the forces if you will, that permit growth and change, but also that which brings destruction and failure."

The look in her eyes intensified, and she began to speak in what I could only assume was the tongue of spirits. "Kom kiñe mew muten deumalei pu antu, pu pullig, ka pu wangelen, pu che, pu mapu." Her stare softened, and she continued to speak. "Everything, Ray, is made of the same thing, the sun, the spirit, the stars, the people, the Earth, we are the truth of everything that exists, and we are connected with everything else."

She released me from her paralyzing stare, took my hand, and placed it around the hilt of the sword. "Your fate lies in her hands, Ray," she said. Then, just as quickly and mysteriously as she had come, she was gone.

I was now standing with one hand holding the sword and the other Laura, who was looking at me bewildered but somehow knowing. There was much I wanted to say and ask, but somehow it just did not seem like I needed to. It was like everything I wanted to know I knew, even though it also felt as if I knew nothing.

When I looked back into Laura's eyes, I saw the same unreasonably reasonable sense of understanding. For the next few moments, we just stood there in silent recognition of what was to come, before we both just smiled at each other and began packing up camp without saying a word.

Chapter 17

Laura and I sat watching the cult as they gathered around the enormous trapdoor that covered nearly every inch of this clearing in the forest. With so many of them surrounding the structure, it was difficult for me to get a good look at it.

Judging from the gap formed at the center of the crowd, I was able to estimate the size to be somewhere around two hundred feet long and maybe seventy feet wide, enough to tell me that whatever it is that lay beneath this gate was not something we ever wanted to get loose.

Most of the cultists were now beginning to take a seated position, and once they were settled, the chanting that began to echo through the trees made me shudder a little. It sounded like something a monk would do with his voice, but at the same time, it was filled with a deep, almost dark, bellowing that was deeply unsettling. On the bright side, with all the cultists now seated, I was able to get a clear view of the monstrous trap door at which they were gathered around.

Made of iron and wood, the door itself resembled that of a medieval drawbridge. The large wooden beams that comprised its center were about four feet wide and ran the length of the door without connection.

"Christ, they must have used whole trees and big ones at that," I said, looking over my shoulder at Laura.

Her eyebrow was heavily furrowed, and judging by the look on her face, she must be having the same sinking feeling in the pit of her stomach as I was. I looked her over for a moment, then returned my focus to the door. The edges were made of some very heavy-duty, and surprisingly, unrusted, looking iron.

The craftsmanship, while enough to strike fear in the heart of any sane person looking at it, was astonishing. And if the sheer size of the door didn't already make you realize that it would be a bad idea to open it, the large iron gate that ran across the top of it with equally detailed work certainly was.

The chanting went on for what seemed like only a few minutes before one of the cultists, dressed in a dark gray cloak, stepped forward and began to recite from a manuscript. "Shit," I said, realizing it was Allister just as he pulled free the amulet from under his cloak. "Where are they?" I said, bringing my eyes to focus on the tree line beyond the cultists and then to the sky.

We had caught up with Eddie and Scarr about three hours ago, and while we had learned from our previous mistake of splitting up, we didn't have a choice this time. Scarr should be swooping in any minute now to sink his claws into that amulet, hopefully taking Allister's hand with it and getting it as far away from here as possible, and Eddie was hellbent on laying a trap for Allister's underling, who was sure to follow Scarr.

Allister lifted the amulet from off his chest and held it out at arms-length. "Ascalementari hash golo."

I should not have been able to hear him at this distance, but his voice was as clear as if he were only a few feet away. He continued to read from the manuscript, and with each passing word, the feeling in my stomach grew worse and worse. Whatever he was reading from was the real deal and whatever was behind that door was about to be on this side of it. I had to, without a doubt, stop him, and I had to do it now.

"Forget the plan," I said, shouting to Laura as I rose to my feet. I turned, reaching to take the sword from her when a loud scraping sound silenced the chanting below, and the gate that shielded the door began to retract itself and move in the direction of the cult's leader.

The cultists sitting closest to the door started to panic, and as they attempted to stand and collect themselves, the ground beneath their feet began to give way, and a number of them fell a good twenty feet to land atop the door.

The gate continued to slide away, bringing more and more cultists to land down on the door. Those that were lucky enough to escape such a fate seemed to decide that sitting so close to their soon-to-be master's path into this world may not have been such a good idea.

They clambered about, desperately trying to stand and backup simultaneously, while those members that crowded in behind them worked to do the same just to avoid being trampled. As for the cultists down on the door, the fear of being stuck was enough to scare some of them to death, with several of them fainting and several others breaking down into tears.

The panic in the eyes of those who remained conscious probably would have brought a smile to my face had it not been for the deafening clang of the gate coming to a stop. The screaming and hollering of the cultists stopped, and for the briefest of moments, the valley grew still, and even the air, with its infinite presence, ceased to exist. It was as if every living creature on earth stopped breathing at once. If not, at least every breath in this valley certainly had.

Then, just as hope might have begun its hesitant return to the hearts of those trapped beneath the safety of the surface, the earth began to rumble, then shake, and large cracks formed around the massive door before spreading outward in every direction, splitting the ground, and releasing fountains of steam high into the air.

The hissing sound that punctured the air was like having a couple hundred Big Boy steam locomotives decompress at the exact same time, and that, coupled with the grinding and cracking of rock as the earth split, was nearly so unbearable that it was all one could do to cover their ears.

"Laura, we have to go now," I shouted, barely able to hear myself over all the commotion.

"I know," she said, at least that's what I thought she said, she was shouting back, but even with our being in such close proximity to each other, her voice was somewhere between audible and strained. She pointed to the sky, and when I looked to see what she was pointing at, I was surprised to see that it was Eddie and not Scarr who was plummeting from above, his aim dead straight at Allister.

"What the hell is he doing?" I yelled. This time, I was sure I wasn't heard. Eddie would not survive the impact from that height, even if he were to hit his target and have Allister absorb the fall. Yet, despite the clear and very present danger of plunging to his death, Eddie appeared to have the most determined look in his eyes.

Allister suddenly slammed the book shut in his right hand and turned to face Eddie. He raised the amulet in his left hand and was just about to open his mouth when a sudden flash of pale green tore past him, and the cultist was knocked to his feet by what looked like a rather hard tail whip that came from the blur that blew past him.

My eyes raced back toward Eddie and got there just in time to see Scarr swoop in, giving Eddie a chance to grab hold of both of Scarr's legs before the pair made a sharp right bank and made their getaway for the forest. It had been a distraction.

When I looked back to Allister, he was already at his feet frantically checking his neckline for the amulet, which, by now, he must have realized had been taken from him, and as that realization set in, he paused. The frustration he was feeling toward not killing us when he had the chance was replaced with anger.

"Get it back," he yelled, his voice somehow still amplified across the valley. I wasn't sure at first how he had managed to keep his voice amplified without the amulet, but when I noticed he was still squeezing the book in his hand, I realized he wasn't going to be entirely powerless when it came time to face off with him.

He turned to a small group of cultists that stood behind him, all of whom appeared to be unfazed by the coming doom, and repeated the order, this time louder and with fewer words. "Now," he shouted again.

This time his order was heeded, and the three cultists took off with giant leaps and high-speed sprints in the direction of Eddie and Scarr. "Whatever you have up your sleeve, I hope it's enough," I said under my breath, wishing my partner good luck.

"Ray," I spun, looking at Laura, who was now pointing back at the door. With all the commotion and the noise, I hadn't realized that the door had already begun to open, and now, as my eyes were back on it, it was too late. The solid wooden doors had split right down the middle and were wide open; the cultists who had once been atop it were now all gone, certainly swallowed by the darkness beneath. Then my eyes came to settle on what Laura had actually been pointing at.

At the top right-hand side, a very large, very smoldering, claw-like hand was digging into the side of the doorway, practically crushing the framework with its might. Just then, another hand shot out from the darkness to come slamming down opposite of the first. When it landed, it sent a streak of forked-like lightning that shot through hundreds of cultists at once, charring them instantly.

"Hell." I turned to reach for Laura and found her already standing close. She pressed the sword in my hand, and for just a moment, as our eyes locked, I felt invincible. I could feel the sword's power pulse through me, but it wasn't the same as before. There was no magnificent light show, no glorious explosion of ice and crystalline dust, no electric misty snakes, and certainly no waves of cold air.

Yet despite the lack of bravado, the power surging through my body was immense. I felt strength like nothing I had ever experienced but was it enough? The hands that had crudely, if not cruelly, made their appearance from the gateway to hell were the least of my worries.

The earth shook even more violently, and the Cherufe, keeping true to its reputation as a dweller of volcanos, a menace of magma and quakes, forced itself free of its prison as it angrily erupted from the earth.

My eyes widened as they sought to take in the monstrosity that rose before me. Ash and earth rose to the sky, dark, and fiery, and electric. Lightning spread through the cloud in all directions, with fierce repetition, and molten rock snaked in and out of the plumb in several places, joining the lightning in one place before disappearing back inside at another.

Then, just when I felt there was no way this could get any worse, something far more fear-inducing happened. The creature hiding inside the plumb made itself known. Massive arms of jagged rock spread on both sides of the cloud, and two piercing eyes appeared followed by a mouth that, when opened, spewed, and spit bright yellow lava between more jagged rock that appeared to function as teeth.

The Cherufe wasn't just a creature made of magma and lightning. It was the magma and lightning, and it wasn't just a dweller of volcanos that caused eruptions. It was the eruptions; perhaps confined or cursed to retreat with every failed attempt at escape.

My mind drifted to the thought of the devastation left in the wake of your average volcanic eruption, and it became immediately clear that this would be far worse. There was no retracting back into the depths. The Cherufe was free of his prison, and we had to stop it now, or this would definitely be the end of the world.

"Laura," I said, using my free hand to caress the soft skin of her cheek before turning her head away from the Cherufe so that I could look her in the eyes once again. There was so much that I wanted to say at that moment, apologies that I felt I owed her, and admittance of my shortcomings, but as we stood there staring at each other, the world literally on fire around us, I found that there was no need for words.

"Let's go, Ray." Her hand let go of the sword entirely as she took my free hand in hers. Her eyes began to glow a brilliant ice blue, and her skin shimmered like thousands of princess-cut diamonds. Together we turned toward the now free evil.

"So, this is it then," I said.

"Yeah, Ray, this is it."

I brought the sword up from my side and grabbed it firmly in both hands. The power continued to force its way through my body, and in that moment, I knew that there was no denying my role in the prophecy. I am Detective Ray Shields, and I am the shield that stands against the darkness.

Chapter 18

"Yep, he's following us, and he's bringing a couple of friends with him." Eddie was hollering over the commotion taking place behind him, and the howl of the wind as he and Scarr flew quickly toward the valley where they had chosen to lay their trap.

"Scraaac." Scarr's reply was simple enough, and Eddie knew he had made his point. One of those things would be trouble enough, but the pair hadn't planned to underestimate Allister again and were ready for the challenge.

"There," Eddie shouted again and chanced, letting go of Scarr's foot long enough to point out where he wanted to be put down. His lack of experience hanging on to a gargoyle as it soared through the sky meant he wasn't quite up to the task and was forced to quickly grasp for Scarr's foot when his request was answered with a quick bank and dive.

"Easy!" Eddie let out a sigh of relief at having both hands back on the wheel, so to speak. "This is my first time, ya know," he shouted.

"Scraaac." Scarr looked back, and when Eddie saw the grin on the gargoyle's face, he knew the hasty maneuver was done on purpose. Eddie smiled back, then let go of Scarr's legs just as they approached the ground.

"You remember what to do, right?" Eddie asked, giving Scarr one last look as he took the amulet from the gargoyle's outreached hand. Scarr nodded once, then leaped atop a boulder, grasping onto a dummy made from Eddie's extra shirt and pants stuffed with branches. "Make sure they don't get too close before you get in range."

"Scraaac," Scarr replied, then in one mighty bound, leaped high into the air and flew back in the direction of the cultists.

"Good luck, buddy," Eddie said under his breath. "We're both gonna need it." He then looked down at the amulet in his hand.

Hopefully, Allister isn't the only one who can use this thing, he thought to himself before thrusting it into his pocket and making his way over to the boulder that balanced preciously on the edge of the cliff. He checked the rope tied to the four-inch diameter log that held the first of the boulders in place and then moved on to check the tautness of another that held back a bundle of stripped logs.

All along the valley's ridge, he and Scarr had placed several traps designed to cause everything from rockslides to full tree-sized logs being dumped down into the valley.

They even set a few that would catapult a rain of bowling ball-sized boulders into the valley when the rope was cut. Scarr had even managed to burrow several two-foot-wide holes in the valley floor that was just deep enough to place three-foot spikes to impale their victims on. Apparently, gargoyles are excellent diggers.

He checked the last of the nearby traps, then drew his pistol and checked his ammunition. He was down to a full cylinder in his revolver with four speed-loaders, one of which was short a bullet he had already used.

"Twenty-nine rounds," he said, sighing as he looked up. Hope it's enough. He watched the horizon as it grew dark from the massive billowing plumb of smoke that rose from where he had left his friends. Gulping, his mind danced with ideas of what horror Ray and Laura were facing, and he began to wonder if splitting up like this was even a good idea.

"Scraaaaaaaaac." His nightmarish thoughts were interrupted by Scarr. His eyes raced to where he had heard the screech, coming to a stop twenty yards to his right. Scarr had flown in low from the tree line, undoubtedly, to ditch the dummy somewhere and race to where the trap was laid. Eddie glanced back over at the trees to see all three of Allister's minions tear free of the forest and bare down on his gargoyle friend.

Scarr stood his ground, digging his claws deep into the earth beneath his feet. "What are you doing?" Eddie said to himself. "Get out of there." Scarr stood firm. The three cultists moved at high speed and were now only fifty yards from the gargoyle. That's when Eddie realized what he was doing. "Ha, a gargoyle after my own heart," Eddie yelled, then gave the rope that held the first trap in place a hefty tug.

Below the sound of the crashing boulder echoed off the valley walls, and the trio that gave chase looked up to see the giant boulder plummeting toward them, bringing with it large chunks of rock and debris as it tumbled down the side of high reaching cliffs.

They stopped to turn around, only to see entire trees cascading down the cliff-side, followed by another boulder and more debris further back. Again, they turned. The only way out now was forward and in their way stood the gargoyle who they had been chasing, and he was unflinching.

The lead cultist ripped his cloak off and revealed himself as the cultist who had killed Camille. Eddie and Scarr both grit their teeth and made ready for the fight while the other two cultists followed their leader's example and tore free their own robes before all three returned to full sprint and bore down on Scarr.

Eddie raced back to the traps that lay ahead and began pulling and hacking away at the ropes without hesitation, only risking glances down to the valley floor as he ran from one trap to another.

Below, Scarr had turned and was flying at high speed just above the ground. He swooped left and right, dodging debris as it fell. Behind him, the trio that gave chase was gaining ground, and it was all Eddie could do to move on to the next trap, giving Scarr as much cover as possible. When he reached the final grouping of traps where the valley curved, he looked down to see the largest of Scarr's pursuers, bow his head and kick it up a gear.

Then, just as quickly, the cultist's face came up as the earth beneath him disappeared, and he fell into one of the ground traps. The others took notice, and realizing what was happening, made way for the valley wall and continued their pursuit. Eddie smirked as the cultist grappled at the edge of the trap, only to have one of the boulders come crashing down on him.

"One down!" Eddie shouted, his voice echoing off the canyon walls to join the choir of tumbling rock and bouncing logs. Scarr spun over, looking up at Eddie, tossing him a little salute, then, with a hard flap of his wings, he thrust himself high into the air. Eddie smiled again and cut the rope that held back the four trees that were bent back like catapults. The boulders let loose, peppering the sky before beginning their descent just short of Scarr to rain their assault on the charging cultists.

The lead cultist had managed to get ahead of the other traps and was scaling the wall on the other side of the valley while his companion sought refuge beneath an outcropping in the valley wall. She might be able to avoid the falling debris, but it would take a great deal more luck to avoid being hit by one of the launched boulders as they hit the ground and tore across the valley floor like a cannonball on a battlefield.

For now, she wasn't the threat. When Eddie looked back to the cultist scaling the wall, he knew this fight was far from over. The slender figure of the man that had killed his sister had already reached the top of the cliff and stood looking at him from across the valley. His brow was furrowed, as if annoyed with the pair for getting the best of him, but it was quickly replaced with a crooked smile and a raised eyebrow. He looked to the sky and began staring down Scarr.

The man brought his hands out to his sides, and like before, his fingers grew long and razor-sharp. He hunched forward, arching his back while his shoulders contorted, and where his shoulder blades once were, two large protrusions began to swell rapidly.

Suddenly, like a pair of balloons put to the needle, the masses burst, and two massive wings tore free of the skin. He reared back his head, stretching out the menacing wings, and let out a maniacal laugh before shifting his stance and leaping high into the air at Scarr.

Scarr returned the gesture by flying backward with a thrust of his wings, simultaneously letting out a war cry of his own, one worthy of being labeled the battle cry of a champion, then he dove straight at his assailant. In an instant, the two powerful figures were entangled. Flashes of claws and batting wings were all that Eddie could make out.

He raised his pistol and took aim, hoping for a shot, but he knew it was useless. He knew that even when the pair separated that they would only charge back at each other at full speed, and he would never be able to get the shot off. And that's precisely what happened. Twice the battling monsters separated, and twice they rushed back head-on, each time releasing that much more fury on their opponent.

Just then, Scarr and the beastly cultist came barreling straight toward Eddie. But just before impact, the brawling ball of flesh shifted, forcing a landing that was more controlled than Eddie would have expected. That's when he caught a glimpse of Scarr's foot burring itself deep into the ground.

It seemed that it was Scarr who was in control, at least for the moment, and it became clear in the seconds that followed when the bulk of the mass slowed, and Eddie watched as Scarr twisted his body in such a way that every muscle in the gargoyle's body flexed, and the cultist was sent hurdling hard past Eddie, smashing into the wall with such force that huge chunks of the rock face broke loose and landed atop him.

Scarr stood panting and only slightly cut up from his encounter, never taking his eyes off his opponent. The man groaned as he rose slowly, letting the rubble fall at his side. Eddie aimed his pistol, this time with a clear shot, but he was stayed by Scarr, who brought his hand up in an awkward manner, palm facing Eddie.

At that moment, Eddie realized two things. One, Scarr had, in fact, taken a bit more of a beating than was immediately apparent. There was a long gash underneath Scarr's right arm, and the blood was only now beginning to seep out. Second, it was also clear that Scarr did not want Eddie interfering in this fight so long as he was still standing.

Eddie nodded. "Fine, but you kill that son of a bitch," he said angrily. "You hear me!" Scarr nodded again, his eyes still on the man in front of him.

"Hahahahaa—cough, cough." The man stood holding his shoulder, his left-wing crippled and all but torn off. "You think she's dead, don't you?" he said between a series of coughs and bloodied laughs. "Well, I suppose she is, in a sense, but if you think Allister would let her off with such a simple punishment, you're wrong."

"Don't you dare play your mind games with me," Eddie screamed, the tears all but hitting the ground as the words tore from his mouth. "I watched her die right there in front of me. When you tore her heart out, you tore every shed of my humanity with it, and when she died, so did I. So don't you tell me she isn't dead, you bastard!"

Eddie's yells were the rawest form of emotion, and it wasn't long before the sadness and anger got the best of him. He stepped forward and raised the pistol once again, ignoring the gargoyle's desire to end this himself, and fired every round in concession, the shots nearly drowned out by the screams of the haunted man until all that came was the click, click, click, of the hammer falling on empty chambers.

Eddie fell to his knees and let the pistol fall to his side. He buried his face in his hands and wept. He wept for all the times he hadn't wept before, when he should have. He wept for all the lost time and unmade memories, and he wept for his sister, who had been through so much only to die at the hands of such a vile creature. He had killed his sister's killer, but instead of satisfaction, all he felt was sorrow.

"Scraeddieee." Eddie felt Scarr's clawed hand on his shoulder, and at that moment, the loss of his sister hurt just a little bit less. Scarr let go, and Eddie watched as Scarr walked over to the dead cultist's body, lifting it by the head and giving it a quick once over before reaping the satisfaction of quickly separating the head from the body and tossing the slack-jawed head of the snake over the valley ledge.

Eddie laughed for a moment, then wiped the tears from his face. He had lost everything, but he had also gained something, a friend. Eddie stood up, letting the thoughts of his sister fade for the time being, and turned to look toward the wake of destruction that they had caused in the valley below.

The entire valley was riddled with debris, and arguably, the traps had brought down far more of the cliffside than Eddie had expected. There was no sign of the third cultist, and he seriously doubted she would have survived. He then looked to the horizon beyond the tree line and saw nothing but darkness.

"I've got a feeling they're gonna need our help," he said, his voice now calm and collected. Scarr stepped up beside him and checked the gash in his side. It was already beginning to heal, and the gargoyle looked at Eddie with all the determination in the world.

"Let's go kick us some Cherufe butt then," Eddie said with a smirk, offering his hand up in front of him as if to say, 'Gargoyles first.'

The gesture was returned with a signature tilt of the head. Scarr began to flap his wings until he was hovering with his feet in arms reach of Eddie. Eddie grabbed hold of the gargoyle, and just as he was about to tell him not to take it easy, Scarr gave a hard flap of his wings and dove off the edge of the cliff, then rose high into the sky, making way toward the next fight.

* * *

"Look out!" I yelled, pulling the sword free of the now lifeless monster that had just placed itself directly between me and the Cherufe. Laura turned and batted away the charging goblin-like beast, with all the strength befitting the warrior daughter of a god, and without hesitation raised her pistol and fired two shots into the toad-like creature to her right.

Even as focused as I was on surviving the onslaught of mythical monsters that had been pouring in on us for the last twenty minutes, this was one of those moments that I made sure to bookmark because I never wanted to forget such a sight.

She brought the pistol back down to her side, and even though there was no light left in the sky, she shone with such intensity that I was convinced the only reason we could see at all was because of the light coming off of her. "I knew Allister wasn't gonna fight fair," she said, making her way back over to my side. "But honestly, pitting his entire zoo against us just isn't responsible for someone who's supposed to be in charge of protecting these creatures."

Laura's compassion for the beasts wasn't without warrant. She had a point. These creatures may have been trying to kill us, but they, like any other animal with an owner, had been taught to behave this way, and it wasn't their fault that Allister was a madman bent on destroying humanity. Nor was it fair that they had been locked up and shown only one way of living, i.e. to serve.

"Ugh," Laura scoffed in disgust, then turned, raised her pistol, and fired another shot, this time hitting a boulder next to a cultist who was standing there shakily holding his own pistol. He promptly dropped the gun and dove behind the rock for cover.

"No, no, it isn't," I said, looking down at the sword in my hand.

Allister was still out there somewhere, and I was very much looking forward to ending his miserable little life, despite my affinity for passivism. The power of the sword seemed to instill in me a deep-seated desire to squash anything that brought a vile taste to my mouth, and Allister was undoubtedly one of those things. "If I have anything to say about it, though, he won't be around much longer anyway," I said.

Laura nodded and looked back at the blackened sky. The air was thick with ash, and any creature that was not of the mythical sort must have opted to make for the hills. The ground around us was littered with one type of monster or another, and at the rate, this was going, it wouldn't be much longer, and Laura and I would be single-handedly responsible for the extinction of a great many species of monsters that were already believed to be extinct.

We were only a couple hundred yards from the Cherufe now, and with the speed that its evil was spreading, we didn't have long before it was upon us, and I would finally be face-to-face with my destiny.

"We better pick our ground fast and stand it," she said, the ferocity in her voice as powerful as the light coming off of her.

I looked at her, and despite her composed appearance, I couldn't help but feel like all this killing was going to have profound effects on her. "Laura, are you sure you want to do this?" I asked.

"Yes, Ray. I'm fine, believe me." She looked at me again and smiled. I returned the gesture and began looking for a place suited to doing battle with a titan.

"Ungatasho ohmalatana," a voice bellowed from behind us. I spun just in time to see Allister gripping the book in one hand while thrusting his other forward from a raised position above his head.

Three car-sized chunks of earth came hurdling toward us at once, each seemingly homed in on me. I raised the sword and made ready to block the incoming projectiles. Laura, however, had a different idea. She stepped between me and what was sure to be my end, then brought one hand up, and with the other, swung a haymaker, driving it deep into the ground at her feet.

The earth rose to create a wall of rock just in time to block Allister's attack. The huge rock wall absorbed the impact of two of the massive projectiles without a problem. However, the third one proved to be the finishing blow, and our earthly shield exploded into a hundred pieces.

I leaped quickly to my right as a piece of shrapnel shot my way, and I was mid-dodge when I felt its presence. Rolling to the side, I looked up to see that the Cherufe, my fated foe, had finally arrived. I looked over at Laura, who was already back on her feet, if not still standing in the same place she initially had been. She was staring up at the titan with fierce determination.

The fear that had once plagued her was no longer present, and at that moment, I understood that while she was very much still my Laura, my well-organized, entirely dependable secretary, who would always be there for me, and for the agency, she was also now, at least in part, nothing less than a warrior goddess.

"You're a fool for coming here, Mr. Shields. You may have bested a few minor beasts, but you can't win this fight. You've only condemned yourself to a quicker death."

I could hear Allister yelling from his position at our back, but I was so focused on Laura, as she stared down the Cherufe, that I didn't care to satisfy my urge to walk over to him and shut him up with a quick swing of the sword. "Either I'm going to kill you, or it will," he continued.

I looked over at him this time, and though it was more out of annoyance than anything else, I had still given him my attention, and so I decided to add a little something just to show him how little I actually cared. Without breaking my gaze, I spat on the ground in front of me and watched as his expression changed from cocky to angry. He turned a few pages in the book until he was satisfied with his chosen method of putting an end to our lives, and he began to chant.

I looked back up at the Cherufe; the ancient evil was now directly above us. The lightning from its body pounding the ground around it was deafening, and the magma that dripped from its mouth made quick work of the earth at its feet, splattering as it fell and burning anything it touched. We were trapped.

No, I said to myself. *This isn't how this goes down.* I gripped the sword tightly, feeling its power as it surged through me. I had to trust that Laura would be able to take on Allister while I did something, anything, to stop the Cherufe.

"Take Allister," I shouted, keeping my attention on the Cherufe. His enormous arm swung through the air, lightning forking through the cloud of smoke and ash left in its wake. In just a few seconds, it would come crashing down on both of us, and it would be all over.

I took off, back in the direction of Laura, chancing one final glance at her, only to see that she was still staring up at the monster that had tormented her for so long. The blue in her eyes was as icy and as cold as the look itself. And still, even with her attention on the Cherufe, she had also raised and was firing her pistol in Allister's direction.

My eyes followed the path her bullet would take and came to land on Allister just in time to see the cultist recoil from the impact of a single round to the chest. The book that was in his hand fell from his grasp, and he crumpled to the floor.

I was now only a few feet away from Laura when the massive fist of molten rock, with its pungent smell of sulfur and hot stone, came crashing down on us. I channeled every ounce of the strength that was inhumanly possible, and with all the courage that was humanly possible, I thrust the sword up with all my might.

The tattoos that had appeared on my right arm when I first handled the sword began to glow, and the sword ignited a vibrant blue just as the monstrous fist made contact with it. The shockwave that came from the explosive force of the Cherufe's assault tore across the countryside. Entire trees were ripped free of the earth, while the earth itself splintered and cracked and tore away.

And yet Laura and I were still alive. The ungodly level of destruction that was unleashed had taken place outside of a thirty-foot-wide, ice-like shield that surrounded Laura and me like a dome. Above, where the Cherufe's fist had been moments ago, there was nothing but a thick cloud of black smoke and fading lightning.

I still held the sword firm in my hand, but I could feel the energy inside of me weakening. And the tattoos on my arms were beginning to look aged. I wasn't sure if the shield had come from the sword or if the sword had simply been a conduit for the shield to travel through; me being the force that created it.

Whatever the case, a great deal of power had been drawn upon to protect us from the Cherufe, and I could only hope that on the other side of that shield, the Cherufe was as affected by the impact as the surrounding area had been.

"Laura!" My mind returned from its state of shock, and I dropped the sword at my side, turning to see if she was safe, but it would seem my worries were for not. Behind me, Laura was floating with her arms out at her side, her hair ethereally dancing weightlessly above her head with her feet hovering just above the ground. The light that had once been a mere shimmer now shown more brightly, and that's when I noticed that the light wasn't confined to her being.

A trail of light had appeared between us. On one end, Laura, in all of her shimmering shiny wonder, and on the other, me, the carriage of a power that was fading rapidly. I looked between Laura and myself, and I could feel her with me. It was as if her life force and mine were intertwined, and there was not a thing in the world that could untangle that union.

"Laura," I said, walking over to her, closing the remaining few steps that kept us apart.

"Ray," she said softly, extending her glowing hand out to me. "It's not done yet, Ray," she said, shaking her head. "We only wounded it."

The light pouring off her dimmed for just a moment before sparking to life at the roots of her hair where, like a trail of gunpowder to a keg, it began to snake its way through every wave and curl, until the fuse had disappeared, leaving in its wake a hair that was so golden-blonde that it would have been hard to look at this woman and not see a goddess.

"In case you didn't notice, I probably just blew that thing up," I smiled childishly at the thought of having annihilated the towering monster with a single swing of my mighty sword, then reached out for her hair.

Laura reached up before I had a chance to touch the golden locks and took my hand in hers. "Your fate is in 'her hands'," she said, emphasizing the final two words. "Ray, it's still alive." She nodded and moved her head a little to the side to look me in the eyes. "I can feel it, and I have to give you all of my power, all of my energy, all of my life if we stand a chance at truly stopping it."

I looked at her for just a second, then with a sudden realization, I tried to tear my hand free of hers, but it was too late. Her grip on my hand was unbreakable.

"Laura, don't do this," I said, my panic showing with every fruitless tug as I continued to try and break free from her. My pleas went unheard and were returned with only a final smile.

Her body burst to life with the force of a thousand suns. And though I should have been blinded by the level of lumens filling the world around me, it didn't even cause me to squint.

Laura, in all her beauty, shone brighter than any painting or poem ever depicting an angel or goddess ever did. The clothing she wore disintegrated against the pureness of the light emitting from her body, and in their absence, only light remained. Perfect, untainted, non-obtruded, celestial light.

The trail between us began emitting a strange golden-blue radiance while at the same time, the tattoos on my arm surged to life, removing themselves from my skin and retracting to their previous mist-like state before wrapping themselves around every inch of my body until I was shrouded with the whirling haze.

"Everything is going to be OK, Ray, I promise." Laura hadn't said anything. She simply floated there, smiling. She was speaking to me through our connection. At first, I was afraid that whatever she was up to was going to cause me to lose her, but somehow, in the calmness of her thoughts, my worries began to vanish. "Just trust me, Ray, like you always have, and everything will be OK."

I nodded my head. "Wha—" I stuttered. "What do I need to do?"

"Do what Ray Shields would do," she replied simply.

Without even the slightest hint as to what exactly I needed to do in order to call on this power that was flowing between us, I was at a loss. But, regardless of my own lack of understanding, Laura had faith in me, she had faith in us, and that meant I had to as well.

I let the sinking worry of losing Laura fade from my mind, and I brought my attention back to the task at hand. I looked down and thought for a minute, trying to come up with anything that might help me kill this monster. Then it hit me. "Do what Ray Shields would do," I repeated Laura's words.

"OK, Ray," I said to myself. "You've got this; you've practiced this a hundred times." I told myself, followed by, "Albeit as a kid." I brought the sword up from my side, raised it high above my head, and in a loud, mighty voice, shouted, "By the power of gray skull, I have the powerrrr."

I could hear Laura softly chuckle, though I wasn't sure if this time it had been through our connection or if she had really laughed out loud.

Suddenly, the mist that surrounded me quickened its already whirling pattern, and I began to lift slowly off the ground. I could feel the power of the sword joining with the external force of Laura's energy, and in that singular moment, I felt invincible. I looked up over my head, my eyes beyond the sword, and with a single thought thrust myself head-on through the ceiling of the icy shield.

The sound of the shattering shield below blended with that of the wind rushing past me as I tore through the sky. When I looked down, hoping to get a lay of the land, my heart sank. Everything was dark, and, so far as I could see, the land that had been unaffected by my clash with the Cherufe was either blackened or ablaze.

I looked for the trail between Laura and myself, but it was gone, and at the speed that I was moving upward, I was only getting farther away.

My eyes began to search frantically for any sign of her when I caught a glimpse of Scarr and Eddie. The pair were on the ground about a kilometer away from ground zero, and I probably wouldn't have noticed them had it not been for Scarr's outstretched wings. He was reaching out for Eddie with one hand and pointing to the sky curiously at me.

When I looked down at myself, I could see why. I wasn't just shooting through the air like a cannonball. The mist whirling around my body was brighter than before and was moving so quickly that I couldn't see any part of myself below the waist. In essence, I looked every bit of what one might imagine a gene free of its bottle might look like.

As the inertia of my mighty thrust into the sky began to wear off and my momentum shifted to a more arched pattern, my eyes finally spotted their target. In the distance, and quite probably directly in my path, the Cherufe's hulking body towered high above the earth.

Even at this altitude, the monumental size of the Cherufe was clear. Not only was it easy to make out the details of its makeup, but the rage fueling the fiery eyes at having suffered such a staggering blow from a creature the size of an ant to it was unmistakably clear.

The Cherufe brought its arms up, throwing them out to its side, thrust its rocky chest forward, opened its mouth as wide as the Grand Canyon, and let out a blood-curdling roar that sent visible waves of heat and destruction tearing through the sky.

There wasn't time to parry the attack, nor could I have dodged them if I wanted to. I didn't exactly have control over where I was heading, and now that gravity was fueling my flight, I was on a collision course with the Cherufe.

I swung the sword furiously in front of me with the arrival of each wave, and to my surprise, as much as my excitement, the audible splintering sound of two opposing elements, if not energies, and the lightning show that followed, echoed across the land and ignited the sky in brilliant explosions of blue, gold and deep red.

The closer I got to the Cherufe, the faster I fell and the faster I had to swing the sword to avoid getting melted away until I was within spitting distance of what was sure to be the final moments of either myself or my monstrous adversary, or perhaps even both.

Suddenly, just as it had done once before when I was so desperately searching for Laura in the mines, the world around me slowed, and everything grew still. I was face to face with the Cherufe, our eyes locked in a heated battle of their own, its mighty presence and the power I wielded in the exact moment of contact.

I can only sorely explain the feeling that surged through me in that decisive moment and the happenings of the moments that would follow. It felt like being gifted with the energy of every particle, of every atom, of every single creature that ever lived on the face of this planet, or any other planet, and having that charge, meet its precise opposite in a display of pure good vs. pure evil.

The world, already still, could not stand any stiller, and as the two opposing forces collided with all the power that could possibly have been mustered by their champions, a grand display of radiance exploded around me.

The sky ignited in a brilliance of color. Like the green fields of the Aura Borealis, waves of blue energy shot across the sky in all directions, dancing vibrant and chaotic. And at the epicenter of the battle, a wall of golden light, shaped nearly like a shield in the hands of a warrior, absorbed the massive red wave of power emanating from the Cherufe.

I could feel the power of the Cherufe pushing back against my own wielded might, and with each passing second, the strength of our two forces was weakening. I wasn't sure how much longer I could hold out, but I was certain of one thing; the Cherufe wasn't fairing any better than I was. I could see the ferocity of its anger through its eyes, and it wanted nothing more than to annihilate both me and the power that had locked it away for so long.

But, beyond that unsurmountable accumulation of rage and evil, there was fear. It was afraid that it wasn't going to be able to defeat me. It feared that this could actually be the end of its very short reign at the surface, and that fear made it weak.

With one final push and every possible shred of resolve that I could bring myself to assemble, I drove the tip of the sword into the Cherufe's rocky skull. It let out a low, rumbling sound that grew louder with every inch gained, and hot steam began to erupt from the wound as the magnificent light emitting from the sword poured in.

The evil contained inside the Cherufe repelled as the golden light made its assault against the darkness, and the Cherufe's mighty body, losing the source of its power, began to recoil. The last of the light in its eyes dimmed, then flickered, and finally wholly extinguished, and the sword in a final display of brilliance ignited and then shattered into a thousand rays of light that shot out in every direction. The thick plumb of ash began to dispel as the light tore through it, and the Cherufe's once-mighty body fell.

It is said that there exists a shield that no evil can penetrate. A shield that will stand against the darkness, sword in hand. Today, Detective Ray Shields stood against the Darkness and won.

Epilogue

Laura and Eddie sat across from each other on the office couch and tossed around the idea of changing the name of the agency to the Ray Shields Monster Slayer Service. "Ya know, boss, it's not a half-bad idea," Eddie said, fully intent on getting me to accept the idea.

"Maybe," I replied, bringing both arms up to rest my elbows on the edge of my desk and clasp my hands together. "But then we'd have to go about building an entirely new client list. And then there's the matter of figuring out what to charge. Not to mention taking out insurance on such a dangerous line of work can't be cheap. I might even have to pull from your salary to make that happen."

Eddie half-cocked his head to the right and rolled his eyes slowly under his brow, as if considering it. "Maybe you're right," he finally said, breaking his moment of thought before adding one final bit to sit on. "But there certainly would be a market for it."

Laura laughed at the remark, then the room grew silent for a few minutes, the three of us clearly reflecting on the happenings of the past few weeks. It's not every day that you get wrapped up in a plot to raise an evil monster locked away beneath a volcano, challenging every belief you ever had about what's real and what's a myth.

And it certainly isn't every day that you are forced to fight dragons, massive dog beasts, and a myriad of other mythological monsters, all in an attempt to stop that evil from being released.

"Ya know, boss," Eddie broke the silence in his usual fashion, then went on to poke fun at all the incomprehensible moments of our situation. "I was wondering, do you think you have any power left in you to grant me a few wishes?"

He was jibing at my appearance while soaring through the sky with a magical cloud of whirling blue light enveloping the lower half of my body. "Ya know," I jibed back. "I think I'm fresh out of power."

"Scraaac," the three of us looked over to see Scarr poised quite comfortably on the office chair that everyone else at the R.S.D.A. had always made it a point to avoid sitting in.

"Hey, it's all yours, pal," I said, both amused and relieved that there was finally a use for the thing.

"All kidding aside," Laura said, bringing her attention back to the matter at hand. "Where do we go from here?"

Her question was well-received, but the truth was, I had no idea what to do next. Allister was gone, at least that's the conclusion we came to as nothing in a quarter of a mile of the impact between the Cherufe's fist and the ice shield was left standing; it would be far-fetched to imagine anyone could have survived such destruction.

The cult was most definitely in ruins, and it wasn't likely that any of the members that survived that day would ever commit back to a life of devotion to the darkness.

"Well," I said. "Maybe we just get back to solving the cases we currently have and give ourselves some time to think about the next step." Laura, Eddie, and Scarr all sat there staring at me. "What?" I said, looking back at them.

"Well," Laura replied, leaning forward and standing up. "It's just that we closed all of our cases right before we left." She grabbed the only folder on the table and walked over, setting it on my desk. "The final write-up for the B. Dalton Case." I looked up at her, and it was all I could do to smile.

Immediately after the sword had erupted and the Cherufe fell, the power that had once surged through me and held me aloft diminished. When it did, and as I slowly sank to the ground, all I could think about was her. Was she safe? Did the remaining part of the shield protect her from the battle that raged just overhead? Was she even alive?

Before everything took place, I had only ever seen Laura as my secretary and friend, a woman that the agency most certainly could not function as effectively without and someone I would prefer to always be around, but I never had feelings for her like I did now.

"Oh," I said, looking around the room. "I forgot about that." I let out a sigh and sank back into my chair.

"What about this?" Eddie said. I looked over to see him holding the small brown leather journal of the cult's once guardian, Valora, in his hand. I furrowed my brow and then bowed my head, briefly shaking it.

"I forgot about that too," I said.

"Well, it's a good thing I didn't." he continued. "You said when this was over, you wanted to try and find him, boss."

"I did," I said, nodding my head satisfactorily at the idea. "I guess since we don't have any other pressing matters," I shot Laura a grin. "We might as well follow up on that." I got up out of my chair and began heading toward the window to play with the blinds. "Let's give Hurston a—." I stopped mid-stride. "Hurston," I said in a low voice.

After reuniting on the battlefield and spending the next three days navigating the ruined landscape followed by the chaos that was fueled by fear and rumor in every city that we passed through, it was when we arrived back at the plane that we began to accept that Camille wasn't the only one we lost in our fight to save the world. The mighty Hurston Hercules flew home without its head pilot that day, and while we still had the beast of a plane, it just didn't feel proper flying around in it without Hurston.

"Ray," Laura spoke softly and placed her hands on my shoulder. "Hurston saved us," she said. "And he did it in a way that only the great Hurston Pierce could pull off."

"The great Hurston Pierce," a voice chimed in from the door to my office. Every head in the office shot in its direction. "Now, I like the sound of that. It has a nice ring to it.

"Hurston, I—" He cut me off before I could even move or finish my sentence.

"Now, now, don't go getting all emotional on me, Ray, it's not like you." He leaned against the door frame and crossed his arms.

"I trust you took good care of my plane," he said, looking over at Eddie and then back at me.

"Yeah. Yeah, it's in fine shape," I replied as the sorrow that had begun to well up in me disappeared, only to be replaced with elation.

"Well, then I guess you've got yourself a ride, after all." The three of us, finally breaking free of the shock at his appearance, headed over to embrace our friend. "It's good to see you again too, Laura," he said, returning her hug and then shaking both mine and Eddie's hands with a firm, meaningful grip.

"And who is this?" he said, looking down at the four-foot gargoyle that stood eagerly behind with his own hand extended.

Stepping out of the way, I chuckled at the sight while Eddie introduced the newest member of the Ray Shields Detective Agency. "Hurston, I'd like you to meet Scarr," he said.

"Scarr, is it?" Hurston bent forward a little and thrust his hand into the waiting gargoyles. "I have a feeling the two of us are gonna get along nicely," he said before starting on the topic of flight. "What do you know about flying with dragons?"

Case Closed